VINCENT DE PAUL: SAINT OF CHARITY

VINCENT DE PAUL

SAINT OF CHARITY

Written by Margaret Ann Hubbard

ILLUSTRATED BY HARRY BARTON

IGNATIUS PRESS   SAN FRANCISCO

Original edition © 1960 by Margaret Hubbard Priley
Copyright renewed, © 1988 by Margaret Priley
All rights reserved
Published by Farrar, Straus and Cudahy, Inc., New York
Published with ecclesiastical approval
Ignatius Press edition published by arrangement with
Farrar, Straus and Giroux, LLC, New York

Cover art by Christopher J. Pelicano
Cover design by Riz Boncan Marsella

Published by Ignatius Press, San Francisco, 2002
ISBN 978-0-89870-870-7
Library of Congress Control Number 2001090562

Printed in India ∞

To Reverend Father Joseph A. Cashen,
another humble man

CONTENTS

1.	The Shepherd Boy	9
2.	The Slave of Tunis	22
3.	Servant of the Poor	35
4.	The First Mission	48
5.	The Time to Run	61
6.	Louise	74
7.	Saint-Lazare	87
8.	The First Foundling	100
9.	Friend of the King	112
10.	A Ride in the Night	124
11.	The Blows of the Hammer	136
12.	The Opening Door	150
	Author's Note	163

I

THE SHEPHERD BOY

THE TINKLE of the sheep bell made a little path through the falling dusk, Vincent thought as he trudged along, a path you could hear instead of see. From many points around a wide circle, other bells were making the same paths in toward the village. Dogs barked here and there. Farther out on the brown plain, a shepherd boy's flute was a thin piping as he trailed his flock home. Before long all the sheep would reach their folds, the tinkling would stop, and the dogs would lap up a drink from the troughs and flop themselves down to rest. The only sound then would be from the piper, who was tagging in late, and perhaps the cow on the other side of the narrow river. She would go on bawling until she was milked. The boy, tramping with his head down, listened to the homely sounds as if he never had heard them before. He had heard them, of course. For sixteen years. The difference now was that he might never hear them again. There would be no flocks or shepherds in the city of Toulouse.

It was odd, though, that he should feel he would not return to Pouy. For more than two years he had been away at school, and he always had come home. But the village of Dax was only a couple of miles down the river. Between here and Toulouse lay 120 miles of dusty road, and it took precious money to hire a horse. The only money, for a time, would be the coins being handed to his father now by shaggy-headed old Anton, who had come from across the river. Anton's laugh rolled up the rise to Vincent.

"A good bargain, eh, Jean de Paul? For your oxen I give you a fine price; my money helps your boy become a priest; the priest prays old Anton into heaven. Good, no?"

Vincent did not hear whatever reply his father made—perhaps a reminder that the price was not so fine—but he saw him turn away. Papa could not bear to see his beloved oxen lumbering off with Anton swinging his whip behind them. Anton was unkind to the creatures he owned, but he was the only one in the village who could pay. Papa had his heart set on the priesthood for Vincent. Nothing else would do. Two years ago, when Father Stephen de Paul, the cousin in the Franciscan Order, had suggested the idea, Jean had taken instant fire. Vincent, nearly fourteen then, had agreed eagerly. Since he was six he had been a shepherd boy and proud of the good care he had taken of the sheep. But make it a life work to follow a dozen sheep? Or to be put in charge of the pigs like his eldest brother, John, or to herd the cattle like Bernard?

"A waste of him!" Stephen had said. "The priesthood offers the only opportunity for a peasant to reach a higher station in life. Let the boy come to us in Dax, and by the year 1600 he will be ready for the university!"

But it was only 1597, and Vincent was ready for Toulouse. At first he had studied hard to please his father and Cousin Stephen; but later, especially in the last year, he knew that even without their encouragement he would have gone on. He had to serve God. Today, out in the hills, he had seen so clearly how it would be: hard work for a few years, tutoring if he could get it because the oxen money would not go far, then ordination and perhaps a return to this home parish. He would fix up the ruined church, help his parents in every way he could, see that his brothers and sisters were well settled in life. . . . Of course he would come back! And he would still be humble. Humility, Father Stephen said, was the virtue from which all others stemmed. Vincent, he said, was learning it well. Father didn't know about the time. . . .

The boy's cheeks grew hot. How he hated that memory! Papa had come to the school, a small, thin man in knee breeches, his rough wool stockings wrinkling down over worn-out shoes, limping as he swung along with his heavy stick. Vincent, seeing him coming, had run and hid. He had been ashamed of his father. The old man, stooped and forlorn, had hobbled away, and he never had come to the school again. But now, to help this ungrateful son, he had sold his precious oxen. . . .

"Oh, I'll make it up to you, Papa!" Vincent said aloud. "I'll make it up, and more!"

The sheep had all straggled ahead, and he ran down the hill into the house yard. Old Black thought it was a game and came tearing up, barking like a pup. Jean caught hold of the top rail of the sheep pen and turned himself around. Vincent was like his father, short and broad, with the typical bowed back of the peasant, his head round, large ears standing out, his nose rather long.

Jean, his brown eyes shining, struck the purse at his waist. "So now we have the money. Nothing stands in your way, my son."

Vincent pulled a long gray splinter off the fence. Now that his father had sold the oxen, he didn't want to take the money. He wanted to be independent, obligated to no one. But he had to get to Toulouse.

"Thank you, Papa", he said, but without enthusiasm.

"Vincent, isn't this what you want, to become a priest?"

"Of course, Papa."

But the answer did not satisfy Jean. He moved uneasily, rubbing his shoulder against the rails.

"I would never push you where you wouldn't want to go. But I've seen signs! You would never bring home the flour from the mill without giving a handful to some poor woman. And the thirty sous you collected to buy the flute, what did you do with it? Gave it to a beggar. Always charity."

"A child's whim", Vincent muttered, embarrassed. He hadn't thought Papa even knew about the thirty sous. He had kept his little hoard carefully hidden under a stone. The day the beggar came along, a terrible, whining creature of bones and rags, it had been around Easter, and Vincent remembered the sermon he had heard in the village church about the thirty pieces of silver. His thirty little sous given to the beggar might help to make up for the awful crime of Judas. But he never had told anyone. If Papa knew about the beggar, he might also know about that shameful incident at school.

"You are no saint, my son", Papa said gently, and Vincent winced. Papa did know! "But you are a good boy, and you will be a good priest. Do the best you can." He laid his hand for a moment on Vincent's arm, then turned and hobbled off to the house.

"Papa!"

But the cry was only in Vincent's heart. Even if the old man had stopped, ready to listen, the boy would not have known how to explain what he felt. But one thing he did know: he would make every day count at school. This was September of 1597. In three years he could be ready for ordination, although he would be only nineteen. A bishop would hardly assign him to a parish until he was twenty-one. But he could teach, perhaps at the university, or return here to tutor Monsieur Commet's wild young sons as he had been doing.

"I'll do *something* to help Papa!" he declared aloud and slapped the rail so hard that his palm stung.

"Vincent! Supper! Mama says come on!" Mary called from the house.

So there would be no chance to talk to Papa tonight, and in the morning he would be leaving. But he'd come back, and then they'd talk. What a relief to shuck his guilty feelings off into the future!

"Run, Old Black!" he shouted. "Last one around the sheep pen's a rotten apple!"

The dog yelped joyfully. The race went into several laps around the pen, and the family had begun their meal before Vincent came in. Quickly he said his grace and pulled his stool up to the table. The pot of hot millet smelled good. Tonight there was meat in it. Everyone was hungry, and the spoons clattered as they met, dipping into the pot.

As the dusk grew chilly outside, the room seemed to gather warmth. The great fireplace with its funnel chimney threw light enough for a winter night. In the corners the big curtained beds were like houses, the hard dirt floor a polished gray in the firelight. There was no

The Shepherd Boy

furniture other than the stools and table, and a workbench where Jean whittled out crude repairs for his farm implements. Over the half door which shut off the cattle shed the cows peered in, one at a time, and the warm animal odor of them was not unpleasant. After supper the family all knelt, each by his own stool, and Papa took his rosary from its peg on the wall and handed it to Vincent.

"Tonight you lead", he said.

The boy cupped his palms to receive the rough wooden beads. Everyone looked at him with new respect, even little Mary, who would be asleep before they finished the first decade. In no other way could Papa have shown his deep regard. No one but Papa ever led the Rosary. It was a scene Vincent never would forget— Jean crouched in the only way he could kneel, with one foot bent under him; Mama sitting back on her heels so Mary could rest against her, the others humped over the stools, the cows looking in, and the dog snoring before the fire. Home, Vincent thought. A priest never had a home. He would never have another.

He expected to lie awake because it was an impressive thing to be spending his last night as a boy under his father's roof, but Vincent was too tired and healthy not to sleep. At dawn his mother aroused him. He dressed quickly in the new shirt and breeches Mama had made. He had no new shoes. Leather was too costly, and the hole in the sole didn't show. Taking the oxen money and the pouch Mama had packed with bread, cheese, and his other shirt, he walked away down the road to the point where he would meet Monsieur Commet. Monsieur was going to Toulouse on business, and he had generously offered Vincent a horse, which he himself would lead home.

And so Vincent headed for Toulouse. He never had been farther away from home than the range of his sheep, thirty miles at the most, and all he knew about the great kingdom of France was what he had learned in school. There had always been war, it seemed, from the time of Charlemagne. Of late years the trouble had been between the Huguenots, as the Protestants were called, and the Catholics. Even the small villages of Dax and Pouy had been drawn into it, and the men, fearful that the Huguenots would raid the church, had attended Mass on Sundays with guns slung about their waists. Henry IV had become a Catholic merely to gain the throne, but under his rule peace had come to the country. Henry was a fairly good king and a good Catholic now. But although the lid was on, the pot still boiled.

Monsieur Commet was a lawyer and a well-informed man, and he spoke of all these things as they rode along. By the time the church spires of Toulouse pointed up over the horizon, four days later, Vincent felt as if he had been gone from home a lifetime.

It was sunset, mild with the balm of September, when they rode through the city gates and along the cobbled street. The buildings were taller than the country boy ever had seen, houses of two stories with a loft above.

Everywhere there were people, hanging over balconies, leaning out of windows, crowding the street, and it seemed to Vincent that they all looked at him with suspicion. If he had been alone he would have slipped off his horse and hidden behind a convenient pile of refuse. But Monsieur Commet was a fine figure in his red-lined cape and hat with the cockade. Erect and not in the least disturbed, he rode straight along to the marketplace, and Vincent followed.

More people, mostly boys, were jammed into the square. Two large groups of young men with dirty faces and torn garments glowered and muttered under the guard of a half dozen constables. Two boys were confined in pillories, which appeared to have had much use. The constables shouted, the boys tried to outshout them, and from the windows of the surrounding shops women and children added their high-pitched racket.

One old fellow with the stained hands of a tanner grinned up at Monsieur Commet.

"Boys! Always in trouble. The gang from Provence got licked by that trash from Guyenne. Next time it'll be the other way around." He squinted at Vincent. "Brought your boy to school here, did you? Well, he'll learn fighting, be sure of that."

Vincent met Monsieur Commet's lifted eyebrow with a grin of his own. He could fight if he had to.

But the lawyer frowned thoughtfully. "Might not some other place be better for you, son? A school where boys study only for the priesthood?"

"No, sir. Father Stephen said there are a couple of schools like that in France, but they're so poor that nobody goes to them."

"But Paris? How about that?"

"No, sir", Vincent said firmly. "Father Stephen says this is the only place for theology."

Monsieur Commet shook his head, looking around at the fracas. "Well, they certainly don't look as if they have their minds on Holy Orders."

"Maybe they're not theological students, sir. They can study anything here."

"Anything or nothing", the tanner said with a cackling laugh. "Got yourself a place to live, son?"

"Not yet, sir."

"Well, they all take lodgers", the old fellow said, dipping a shoulder toward the far side of the square. He winked at Monsieur Commet. "Tell him to keep his mind on his books; he'll get along."

In the weeks that followed, Vincent applied himself so hard to his studies that he got along very well, although there were many distractions. His living quarters were poor, and he often was cold. The students were a wild young lot, roaming the streets and brawling all night. Young renegades, chased by a constable, would take refuge in Vincent's room, for it soon became known that de Paul was one of the small number who had come here to study, and they knew he would be sitting reading by the light of his candle. If they appeared at classes at all, they would be bruised and sleepy, in no frame of mind to listen to lectures, and when examinations came up they would pester Vincent for help. One young wastrel, named Goddard, attached himself so fondly that he and the peasant boy became roommates. Vincent was worried about this new distraction at first. But Goddard's roistering kept him out so much that he was no bother, and he was always cheerful when reminded to pay his half of the rent.

By Christmas, Vincent could write to his father that his instructors were pleased with him and that he was doing well. There was no reply. After the New Year he wrote again, and this time when he received no answer he sent a letter to Monsieur Commet, asking news of the family. Toward the end of February the reply came. Jean had been ill, and Mama had not wanted Vincent to know about it for fear he might leave school and come home. But now they could tell him, for there was nothing he or anyone else could do. Papa was dead.

Vincent was stricken. Papa had left a will stating that the family must help financially until the ordination: that was how important Vincent's education was to Papa. He had sold his cherished oxen; he had denied the other children the small comforts and treats they might have had; now he even directed from the grave that they go on helping. And Vincent once had been ashamed of him. Over and over, the boy lived through that shameful incident at Dax. Not even Goddard's foolery could lift him out of his grief, for this was a sorrow that would remain with him the rest of his life.

Finally Vincent wrote a long letter to Monsieur Commet. There was no use addressing it to Mama this time, for he wanted a reply, and no one at home could read.

"I am studying harder than ever," he wrote, "and I have enough money to live on now because I have found some tutoring to do. Please do not worry about me. Tell Mama not to be concerned about me any more. Tell her whatever money she gets for the wool she should use for the others. My sisters will marry, and she will need it for them."

It was not exactly true, when he wrote the letter, that he had found work as a tutor. But within a few weeks he was going regularly to Buzet, a village fifteen miles from Toulouse, where he had agreed to teach two sons of nobility. Soon word spread that he was an excellent teacher, and several more parents asked that he enroll their sons. Finding that the journey took too much time from his studies, he moved his little school bodily to Toulouse, where he housed himself and his students in one building. This was a great sorrow to Goddard, who had not wanted to lose his roommate. The school was successful enough to support Vincent through ordination.

On September 19, 1598, Vincent was ordained a subdeacon by the bishop of Tarbes, and on December 17 he became a deacon. Two years later, he was ordained to the priesthood. He was not quite twenty years old.

He could have returned to Pouy to say his first Mass,

The Shepherd Boy

and perhaps he would have done so if his father had been living. But the journey would be expensive, and he planned to continue his studies at the university. In a small chapel dedicated to the Blessed Virgin, high on a thickly wooded mountain near Buzet, Vincent offered his first Mass with no one but the old caretaker and a priest in attendance.

The shepherd boy had come a long way from Pouy.

2

THE SLAVE OF TUNIS

THE CITY OF MARSEILLES was in a holiday mood on that summer day of 1605. Laughter, the music of flutes and drums, the loud chanting of street hawkers, and the general happy bedlam of a crowd all floated down to the quay where the two young men stood talking, one in the black cassock of a priest, the other wearing highly fashionable red.

"We'd be taking too great a chance, and you know it, Goddard", Vincent said. "The Gulf is infested with pirates. I wouldn't care to be on a ship they might attack." And his alert brown gaze slipped between the brightly colored sails of the vessels packed around the moorings and out to the far blue horizon that was the Mediterranean.

"I agree", said Goddard, flipping the red cape. "Do you think I want to be in the middle of a fight?"

"Yes", said Vincent, and they both laughed. It was good to be together again, for they had not met in a year.

In 1604 Vincent had received his degree, and since then he had tried hard to lay out some direction for his life. Having been promised the parish of Tilh, near his own home in the Landes, he had gone clear to Rome to defend his right to it against the claims of another young priest. He had lost his case. Returning to Toulouse, he had received another promise of a good benefice, and on this business he had gone to Bordeaux. Again he had acquired nothing but debts. He was on the point of starting up a school when an unexpected legacy was left him by an old lady he barely knew in Toulouse. The property was small, but the sum of three hundred crowns was owed her by a rascal who had run off to Marseilles to escape his debt. Vincent had followed him here and had him arrested, and the fellow's family had paid the amount to get him out of prison.

"You have the three hundred crowns", Goddard remarked, going back to the story Vincent had just told him.

"I also have debts. I rented a horse to come here."

"But you sold the horse to raise money to have the ruffian arrested."

Vincent's face flushed clear up to his shaven tonsure. "I'm not dishonest, Goddard. I'll pay the owner as soon as I get back to Toulouse."

"Oh, but certainly! And the cheaper you travel home, the more money you'll have left over. So we go with my friend, the captain of the *Louise*, across to Narbonne, and from there we can easily get up to Toulouse."

"You remember what happens to the luckless wretches caught by the pirates—they're sold into slavery."

"So we will not be luckless", said Goddard.

Vincent was secretly happy to be persuaded. A journey by ship would be high adventure.

Goddard's friend the Captain was jovial over collecting two more fares, and in the middle of the afternoon the *Louise* opened her sails to the wind and pointed her prow toward the open sea. But she was barely out of sight of land when the lookout in the crow's nest broke into a sudden shouting, waving his arms to the west in such great excitement that he seemed in danger of toppling out of his canvas basket.

"Pirates! Pirates!"

"It couldn't be, not this close to shore!" Goddard exclaimed.

But already a ship appeared to be rising up out of the water, and a little distance back, two more. They bore the square rigging of the brigantines, the pirate craft of the Barbary Coast.

The Slave of Tunis

"To the oars!" the Captain roared. "Bowmen, see to your arrows!"

Within minutes, it seemed, the three brigantines had surrounded the *Louise,* and the air was barbed with arrows. Fierce men with naked brown backs and rings in their ears were leaping aboard. One caught sight of the two young men on the captain's dais and with a wild yell waved his cutlass. Vincent closed his eyes. He had received an arrow in the leg, but the pain was not nearly so great as the anguish of hearing Goddard's cries. Waiting for the cutlass to cleave his own skull, he prayed humbly.

Afterward, the memory of that terrible incident was never very plain. Vincent knew that the pirate jerked the arrow out of his leg, bandaged it roughly with a yellow scarf, and shoved him after the others who were being forced to cross on a narrow plank to the deck of one of the brigantines. Goddard had been cut to pieces. Perhaps his own black robe had saved him.

In the days that followed he would wonder many times whether he should be thankful that his life had been spared. The pirates were brutal. For nearly a week the ships prowled the Mediterranean, hunting more victims, but when none were found they set sail for Tunis, on the notorious Barbary Coast. Before leaving the ships, each prisoner was stripped of his own clothing and attired in a pair of white linen trousers and a cap. Now there was nothing to distinguish the young priest from the others.

"God help us, Monsieur. You could get the galleys or the marble quarries same as us!" a big sailor groaned. "He's too skinny", said another. "He wouldn't last a day. He'll go for a house servant."

"What are you talking about!" a third snapped. "We're French citizens! There's a king's consul in Tunis to keep things safe for the traders! They wouldn't dare sell us as slaves!"

"Then why are we rigged out for the auction block?" the first rejoined. "What's to keep them from swearing we were taken from a Spanish ship? There's not a conscience among the lot of them!"

The big sailor, Vincent knew, was only too correct. Chained neck to neck, the captives were herded in a long line from the deck to the burning sand, then marched clear around the town. Vincent could not help limping. The arrow wound was still very sore, and the sand scorched his bare feet. Long before he was herded with the others to the marketplace, his shoulders were red from the sun.

At the market, the prisoners were each given a trencher of stew.

"Eat, Father", whispered the man beside Vincent. "We've got to eat. If they think we're sick we'll be dumped in the bay!"

But the trenchers were whisked away almost immediately, and the selling began.

Vincent was bought by a fisherman, a rough fellow who looked like a pirate and roared with anger when his

The Slave of Tunis

slave became miserably seasick on their first fishing trip. Luckily for Vincent, he was sold then to an alchemist, an old and mild-mannered man who saw at once what a prize he had obtained. In the walled garden the new slave was given his own little hut under a palm tree, and while he kept up the fires in the dozen furnaces where experiments were being tried, the alchemist would talk to him in excellent French.

"For fifty years I have searched for the Philosopher's Stone", he said one day. "You know what the Stone is, of course, Vincent?"

"I know you believe it will have the power to turn baser metals into gold, sir."

"And to prolong life so men can live for hundreds of years." The old man paused, for they had been over this before. "You don't believe this is possible?"

"Only God can do such a thing."

The alchemist sighed. He wore a simple long robe of plain white, and with his long beard he resembled a patriarch of the Bible.

"I would give you wealth, Vincent", he said. "I would teach you all the secrets I know if you would accept Mohammedanism."

"No, sir", Vincent replied quietly. He had made the same answer many times in the past weeks. He wore only a white loincloth, and he was as brown as any native, but inwardly he had not changed.

"Your God has deserted you", the old man said.

"Indeed, he has not, sir."

"Then why does he not snatch you up and fly with you back home?"

Vincent poked the fire under the oven. "Why do you want a fire as hot as this, sir?"

"To melt the metal I placed in the oven and remove the impurities."

"That's what God is doing to me, sir. He is trying me out in slavery so nothing will be left in me but the purity of my faith in him."

Vincent moved to the next furnace. He liked the old alchemist. He even enjoyed the work he was required to do, and if he had been born a slave, he sometimes thought, he might have been happy. But always there was the agony of yearning to fulfill the vocation to which he had been ordained, and his prayers for release to the Blessed Virgin were never ending.

The summer of 1606 slipped along to an August day when the alchemist came slowly along the path under the palm trees and stood in silence beside Vincent. He looked very old and tired.

"The Sultan has called me", he said quietly. "He has heard of my work, and he has bidden me go to Constantinople. It is a great honor." He laid his hand on Vincent's brown shoulder. "I am not going to sell you, Vincent. My nephew will keep you for me until I come back. Then we'll go on with our work."

Vincent never saw him again. He heard later that the kindly old man had died on the way to Turkey. The nephew, a scapegrace who cared nothing for his word, became alarmed when the news came around that the king of France was sending an ambassador with special permission from the Grand Turk to rescue the Christian slaves. Before the ambassador even arrived in Tunis, Vincent was sold by the nephew to an apostate French priest, who took him off into the mountains.

Here, Vincent came very nearly to despair. In the city of Tunis he had been at least within range of the French merchant ships in the harbor. Now, back in the hot, arid highlands he felt as if he were buried alive. He was put to work as a laborer in the fields, digging out the tough African weeds with a primitive hoe. But the torment of his blistered hands and aching back was small compared to his anguish of spirit. For the first time he felt completely abandoned. His prayers became as automatic as his chopping of the weeds. He could not know that God was stirring the fires of purification to a white heat before preparing to bank them.

Vincent little suspected that the first step of his deliverance was at hand when he looked up one afternoon to see one of the wives of his owner watching him from the cover of a thorn bush. The Frenchman, William Gautier, had three wives. He had been a Franciscan friar and was captured by pirates and brought to Tunis, where he bought his freedom by becoming a Mohammedan. This girl, young and pretty, was the newest of his wives. Yesterday she had come to the field and watched for a while. Today she came closer, not with boldness but simply because she wanted to see this man from the far-off land.

She had carried a jar of water on her shoulder, and now she swung it gracefully to the ground.

"You may drink", she said. Gautier had taught all of his wives to speak French.

Gratefully, Vincent took the cup she held out to him. Then he bent again to his work. But the girl did not leave. He heard the delicate tinkle of her bracelets as she settled herself in the shade.

"Tell me about yourself, please?"

Vincent smiled faintly. The story of his life would not bear recounting. Wishing in some manner to obey, he began to sing the psalm he had often recalled through the past days, "We wept when we thought of Zion." Then, because the girl appeared to be touched, he sang the beautiful prayer "Hail, Holy Queen, Mother of mercy, our light, our sweetness, and our hope."

The young wife wiped her tears away. "After the exile you will reach heaven? Tell me about it."

That was her request all the afternoon, "Tell me about it." She sat listening until the bell summoned the slaves from the fields.

"Tomorrow I will come again", she said. "But this paradise of yours, if it is so glorious, I cannot understand why our husband gave up his chance of going there. I am going to ask him about it, for I believe he has made a great mistake in deserting his religion."

Vincent was faintly uneasy. Gautier knew very well the terrible error he had made, and he might not care to be reminded of it through a slave.

The next morning, however, the Frenchman appeared in the field.

"You're right", he said to Vincent. "I should have remained a slave until God would deliver me. My young wife—a Mohammedan!—has convinced me that I must return to the Church, even though she knows the only way I can do it is to escape from here and desert them all. I'll do it. And I'll take you with me back to France!"

But ten months went by before Gautier kept his promise. On a hot June night the two men alone put out to sea in a small skiff. Pirates still ranged the Mediterranean; quick summer storms could whip up in minutes; even a playful whale could wreck so tiny a boat. But the passage was made in safety, and soon after dawn on June 28, 1607, the landing was made at the old rallying point of the crusaders, Aigues-Mortes.

Vincent wept when he felt the soil of France once again under his feet, and Gautier was so overwhelmed that he knelt in the street. Although the hour was early, a crowd gathered around these two brown foreigners in the biblical robes who wept and embraced one another.

"Are they crazy?" a child asked.

Several dogs started a fight, and in the general excitement Vincent and Gautier slipped away.

"First let's visit a church", said the Frenchman. "And then we must buy ourselves some clothes. I brought plenty of money with me."

"If you would lend me the price of a cassock", Vincent began.

"Lend! Man, I'll buy you a dozen cassocks! Didn't you rescue my soul from hell?"

Properly dressed, riding the horses Gautier had hired, they ended their journey at Avignon that night and presented themselves at the palace of the Papal Vice-Legate.

Vincent had made a wise choice in going to Monsignor Peter Montorio, who was fascinated with their tale of adventure. The next day he would receive Gautier back into the Church. Then, upon the arrival of the new Vice-Legate, who would replace him at the end of his term, he would take them both to Rome, where Gautier could enter the Fraternity of Saint John the Divine, a penitential convent of the Franciscan Order. Vincent, whose knowledge of alchemy delighted Montorio, would remain with the Monsignor, and correspondence would be started with the bishop of Dax in regard to a benefice.

During the two years of his slavery, Vincent had put himself completely into the hands of God. Through the next months he had need of that patience. Documents came from the bishop of Dax, but the signatures were not right, and the papers had to be returned. When the same thing happened a second time, Vincent knew it was deliberate.

"But I can't blame the bishop", he said to Monsignor Montorio. "I've told him almost nothing of my experiences in Tunis. So far as he knows, I might have been doing something most degrading to my priesthood. And yet how can I explain?"

The Monsignor understood. Alchemy was thought by many to be a tool of the devil, and the cautious bishop of Dax was among that number.

"You are continuing your theological studies. You seem to love Rome", Montorio said. "But you are not happy here. Why, Vincent?"

"Because I am an exile from France, sir. I was not ordained for this."

"There is a way you can return to France. I haven't mentioned it because I was hoping not to lose you." He paused, smiling at Vincent's eagerness. "Our king, Henry IV, has several ambassadors here, negotiating with the Holy Father to form an alliance that would protect us from the growing power of Austria. Now they need a messenger to carry word back to the king of what they have accomplished. It is too secret even to be written. The messenger would have to talk with them and then with the king." Again Montorio paused to smile. "I have recommended you, Vincent."

Vincent grasped the Monsignor's hand, for he could not speak. He had promised himself that he would not return to France without a benefice, but God was ordaining it otherwise. Through the medium of a Mohammedan girl he had brought his slave to freedom. Now he would return his servant to France as a messenger to the king. Vincent was twenty-eight and had been a priest for nine years, yet he never had exercised the duties for which he was ordained. If at times he wondered why God should permit this apparent waste of faculties, he did not question his power to do so. Even in these early years, before any of his work had begun, Vincent had come to realize that in having no will of his own he would be doing God's will.

With great expectation he set out for Paris.

3

SERVANT OF THE POOR

ON A FEBRUARY DAY of 1609, Vincent rode through the gates of the great white wall built around Paris by Philip Augustus, through the narrow cobbled streets, across the Little Bridge to the Island of the City, and into the courtyard of the Palace Royal. So urgent did he feel his mission to be that he had not paused even at a well to wash the grime from his face, and he was ushered into the presence of King Henry IV still wearing the heavy cloak and scarf he had been forced to buy to protect him from the cold as he came north.

He was with the king a long time, and the candles were lighted in the drafty old halls when he finally took his departure. Some of the wide open doors let out the sounds of laughter and women's voices, but Vincent did not glance into the firelit rooms. Court life had no appeal for him. He was very tired, and he still must find lodging for the night. The king had offered him hospitality, but he had declined. He did not belong here.

"Who are you?" a young voice demanded suddenly.

Vincent paused. Hurrying along with his eyes cast down, he had not seen where the boy had come from. He was a lad of about eight years old, curly headed, dressed in velvet of a rich red that set off his impudent face. On one gloved wrist he held a small, hooded falcon.

"I said, who are you?" he asked again.

"I am a priest, attending to my business", Vincent said quietly. "Who are you?"

"The dauphin. Some day I'll be king of France. I'm a very bad boy." And his eyes danced as he said it.

"Then you should mend your ways, or you will be a very bad king", Vincent said, but he had to smile.

The young dauphin flicked a fingernail against the bird's yellow skin. The falcon let out a sharp squawk, and the boy, laughing, spun around with the bird held high.

"She hates me! I pull out her feathers, and she rips my glove to pieces! But she can't fly. Do you know why?"

"Because she can't see. Without the hood she would be free. You shouldn't torture a blind thing."

The boy stopped laughing. Soberly he sidled over to Vincent. "I like you, sir. For you, I'd be good. Couldn't you be my tutor?"

"I'm sure you already have a tutor, my lord. I believe he is coming down the hall."

Young Louis whirled. Then, laughing, he darted away in the opposite direction from the harried-looking priest who was advancing with several books under his arm. The priest nodded to Vincent.

"Purgatory is no imagined state to me", he said. "I'm in it!" And he was off at a jogging trot, trying to catch up with the dauphin.

Out in the courtyard, Vincent took his horse from the groom. His twofold mission had been accomplished: the message was delivered to the king, and he himself was once again in France. But now, like our Lord in his wanderings, he had nowhere even to lay his head.

Gray days came now for Vincent. God, having brought him back to France, apparently had no immediate plans for him. The young priest had very little money. He found a poor room and shared the rent with a judge from Sore who was too stingy to live in a better place. He seldom saw his roommate, for he spent many hours a day working in the Charity Hospital, a loathsome place staffed by four Brothers of Saint John of God. Vincent was ill frequently, and his small funds were dwindling to the point when there would soon be none, but he was not concerned about his physical well-being. He was anxious only to use the faculties of his priesthood, and at the hospital there was ample scope. Patients lay three and four in the beds, the dying and the plague stricken and the recovering ones all in together. Refuse was thrown on the floor; food was whatever could be scraped together. Through this terrible place twenty-five thousand patients would pass in a year, most of them carried out to the cemeteries.

Here Vincent came every day with his gentle hands and quick words of kindness. No task was too repulsive for him. In the bodies of the sick he was serving Christ. He was outside emptying a basin in the gutter one day when a priest glanced at him and paused. The stranger was about Vincent's own age and attired like him in a plain black cassock.

"So you are the one", he said, smiling. "You cared for the brother of my servant here. You didn't ask him to make his confession before you washed his face, either. That pleased him so much that he made a very good confession. He couldn't tell me your name."

"Vincent de Paul, sir."

"I am Pierre de Bérulle. I live in this neighborhood."

Vincent had to smile at the modest remark. He had heard of de Bérulle, one of the finest orators in Paris, already spoken of as a cardinal. He was often to be seen around the court of Queen Mother Marguerite, a stone's throw away in the suburb of Saint-Germaine, yet this association did not dim his interest in the poor. His voice was often raised in condemnation of the loose practices of the clergy, a subject shunned by most priests. What a friend he would be!

"What is your benefice, Vincent?" de Bérulle asked.

"I have none. I am a native of Pouy, the son of a peasant. I expect to return there very soon."

"Then the bishop of Dax has something for you?"

"Nothing, sir", Vincent began, but he was interrupted by a gentleman who swept around the corner with such velocity that several bits of paper flew up in the breeze. It was Vincent's roommate, the judge from Sore. Disregarding de Bérulle, he stamped up to Vincent and shook his stick as if he intended using it as a weapon.

"Where is my money?" he demanded. "My four hundred crowns I left in the cupboard! What have you done with it?"

Vincent was too stunned to do more than mumble that he knew nothing about the four hundred crowns.

"Who else could have made off with my money?" the judge stormed. "I'll have you arrested!" He tramped away, then turned and spat out "Thief!" before he disappeared around the corner.

Vincent was so ashamed he felt ill. The apothecary's boy had come this morning with medicine, and he had taken a glass from the cupboard. Perhaps the rascal had taken the money also. But there was no proof. The situation was embarrassing for de Bérulle. He said good day and went on, leaving Vincent in the company of a pigeon pecking at something between the cobblestones.

It would be six years later that the boy, brought up before the judge for stealing, would confess to having taken the four hundred crowns, and the judge then would write Vincent a letter of sincere and lengthy apology. But there was no one to help him now. Going sadly back to his work, he reflected that God seemed to be requiring every sort of failure from him. De Bérulle, who might have become a treasured friend, would not give another thought to a priest who was a thief. Whatever chance he might have had to secure a benefice in Paris had now been blown to bits by the judge. Vincent remained late at the hospital, returning to the dank little room only after he thought the judge would be in bed. But the gentleman had packed up and departed. Vincent sat down and wrote a letter to his mother, telling her he would be coming home. He could at least be another pair of hands to plow the fields.

Several days passed, and although Vincent went his familiar round, giving the judge ample opportunity to have him arrested, no constable appeared. The story, however, was being spread. Conversations were hastily cut off at his approach; glances were quickly withdrawn when he looked up. Vincent the thief was gaining a fame never earned by Vincent the priest. Then, on the morning he had set for his departure from Paris, a note was brought by a page boy in the glittering livery of Queen Marguerite's household. Vincent was to come to her palace that afternoon to receive his appointment as her almoner.

The fine paper fell from his hand, and a shivering passed over him worse than the ague. For many more years, until his future lay before him in so certain a channel that even he could have no doubt, he would experience this terrible reluctance whenever any new proposal came up. He was on his knees by his bed when there was a quick knock. Then the door opened, and Pierre de Bérulle was in the room. Grasping Vincent by the hand, he pulled him to his feet.

"Congratulations! Now we'll be meeting often!" he cried, but at the sight of Vincent's face his tone changed to dismay. "You wouldn't turn it down! Oh, no!"

"I'm not worthy. I'm not an administrator. I've done a little teaching, but nothing to prepare me for—"

"Nonsense!"

"Pierre, I'm a peasant! I don't belong in royal circles!"

"Does the son of a rich man know the value of money?" de Bérulle demanded, but immediately dropping his oratorical air, he sat down on the bed. "Listen, Vincent, carefully. Paris is infested with beggars. You know that. Some of them are perfectly able-bodied men; some are sick and old; about half are women and children—all together ten thousand or more! The king is going to drive them out of the city unless something better can be done. If distributed wisely, the Queen Mother's alms can save the situation. You are the one to do it, Vincent."

"Banishing the beggars from Paris would only send them into the country", Vincent said. "In a few months they would all be back. But if we could put to work those who are able to work, separate the aged and the children...." He paused, shrinking again. "I couldn't live at court, Pierre!"

"You wouldn't have to. I'm getting together a company of priests, intellectuals—I'm calling it the Oratory. It's to be like those places Philip Neri founded in Italy, but independent from them. So far I have only a house and two men. Come and live with us. I promise you, if you've taken a vow of poverty, you'll have no trouble carrying it out!"

Vincent laughed. The shivering was gone. De Bérulle jumped to his feet, and they shook hands, pounding one another on the back like schoolboys.

"You do believe I can do this, don't you, Pierre?" Vincent asked a final time.

"I *know* you can!"

Through the next few years the same question would be asked and the same answer given many times. The wisdom of de Bérulle would come to be Vincent's guide.

As the Queen Mother's almoner, Vincent became a familiar figure around Paris. At any hour of the twenty-four he might be found in the old saltpeter workings or the ancient stone quarries, which had become the haunts of beggars. Among these forgotten people he made more friends than he did at court, where he spent as little time as possible. Religion, and therefore charity, had become an active thing for Queen Mother Marguerite herself, but her ladies accepted it mostly as another form of entertainment. Her small court was a gathering place for writers, musicians, poets, and artists. The headstrong young dauphin was often to be seen romping through the halls, being spoiled by everyone who wanted the favor of Marguerite. None of the gaiety appealed to Vincent. Hurrying along, looking to neither right nor left, he managed to keep an invisible wall around himself, and no one tried to scale it.

On the fourteenth of May in that same year, 1610, Henry IV was assassinated, and the dauphin became King Louis XIII with his mother, the slovenly and coarse Marie de' Medici, as regent to rule until he would come of age. With a peasant's reverence, Vincent mourned the untimely death of his king, but his little routine was not altered. God was at last making use of him, and he knew the happiness of fulfillment.

His contentment, however, ended suddenly with what he felt to be the strangest crisis of his life. At Marguerite's court he had made one friend, a doctor of theology who had preached all over France and was famous for his knowledge of the doctrines of the Church. Now a terrible affliction had come to him. He was so assailed by doubts that his faith had been destroyed, and he had no belief in anything. All he could do, he told Vincent, was to keep his mind as blank as possible. When he tried to pray, apparitions appeared to him, so horrible that he had an impulse to throw himself out of a window to escape from them.

"Then do not try to pray at all", Vincent advised the unhappy man. "Point toward Rome as an act of faith. And I will ask God to visit your doubts upon me instead of you."

The doctor's mind cleared, and he was once again able to pray.

But now God exacted payment from Vincent. Unable to pray, afraid to sleep because of the awful nightmares, his nights became so filled with terrors that he would go out and roam the streets of Paris. Often he walked until dawn. But he felt no rebellion. This was the bargain he had made with God. He wrote out the Apostles' Creed and pinned it over his heart, asking God to take his touching of the paper as an act of faith. More than a year went by, and the little folded paper had to be renewed many times. Vincent spoke to no one of his torment. Stolidly he kept to his routine as almoner and went whenever he could find time to the Charity Hospital.

It was in the hospital, working over a patient, that the answer came to Vincent. He must serve the poor. Not for an hour when it was convenient, but for his entire life he must serve the poor. Instantly, his tormented state left him. In the flash of a second, he knew he could pray again.

He went first to the chapel of the Oratory, and then to Pierre de Bérulle. Pierre must have found it hard to ask no question through this tortured year. Vincent told him the whole story.

"I have found myself!" he finished. "Myself and God.

But what shall I do now, Pierre? Continue on as almoner? Is it enough?"

De Bérulle shook his head. "No. You're ready now, Vincent."

"Ready for what?"

"Clichy. You know the place, only a short distance out of Paris. The present pastor has been wanting to come to us. If you really want to serve the poor, Vincent, you'll get your wish there!"

Vincent was delighted. He found the church in ruins, the people desperately poor and indifferent. His first act was to ask a few of the women to come and help him clean the church. On Sunday, curiosity drew enough people to Mass to fill the small number of benches. Through the week he cajoled the men into building more benches, and the following Sunday all the seats were taken. Soon everyone was talking of Father Vincent, who never scolded; who taught their children catechism; married, buried, and baptized; who was never in too much of a hurry to talk or sit with the sick and yet accomplished such an amazing amount of work. The women, coming to his door with a loaf of bread or a shirt they had washed for him, peered inside, saw the extreme cleanliness of the bare little place, and hurried home to scrub their own poor houses. When the church was renovated and even supplied with stained-glass windows and a new baptismal font through the generosity of certain acquaintances of Vincent's in Paris, the pride of the villagers was outdone only by their piety.

"Even the Pope himself is not so happy as a parish priest in the midst of such kindhearted people", Vincent said one day to Cardinal de Retz, the archbishop of Paris, who happened to stop on his way through Clichy. "I think not even you, my lord, are as happy as I!"

"Then you are indeed blessed", said the cardinal. "Not everyone in this world is so fortunate as to find the niche God meant for him."

It was a blow to both Vincent and his parishioners when a summons came from Pierre de Bérulle.

"The good work you have done in Clichy can now be carried on by a substitute", Pierre wrote. "You may still be pastor in name and continue to visit the parish when you have the time, but you are ready for a new field. I have found it for you in the household of Phillippe-Emmanuel de Gondi. His sons are in need of a tutor. Your successor will be in Clichy by the end of the week."

Cardinal de Retz was a brother of de Gondi. Did his short visit to Clichy have anything to do with this appointment?

"Oh, Pierre, what are you thinking of?" Vincent sighed to himself. But he had no intention of disobeying the order. For some time yet, de Bérulle would be his spiritual guide.

The people wept and protested; some even shouted in anger when they heard their pastor was leaving. A delegation of men came to his house, declaring they would lock him in so he could not go. To all of them, Vincent was gentle. He regretted leaving everyone, but most of all young Anthony Portail, who had been studying with him as a first step toward the priesthood. Anthony was so painfully shy that he might desert his vocation rather than go to school. God would have to see to it that he didn't.

Vincent gave away his meager possessions, keeping only the few books and pieces of clothing that he could pack in a hand barrow. Then he said good-bye to Anthony; blessed the shouting, milling crowd, which actually was a mob at this moment of departure; and set out for Paris, trundling the barrow. He couldn't see the road through his tears.

Pausing once, he looked back. Two women were fighting over an old cap he had left, worrying it between them like a bone. Young Anthony leaned against a tree, his face hidden.

Turning away, saddened to his very soul, Vincent trundled the barrow on toward Paris.

4

THE FIRST MISSION

VINCENT'S THOUGHTS were confused on that lonely walk from Clichy into Paris. Pierre knew of his vow to serve the poor, yet here he was taking him away from that service and setting him in the middle of a wealthy and fashionable household to tutor a boy who would probably become Cardinal de Retz, archbishop of Paris, since that post had been held by the House of Gondi since 1570, and another who might be appointed general of the king's galleys, like his father. Vincent de

The First Mission

Paul, son of a peasant, teaching the future great nobles of the land! What *was* Pierre thinking of?

But Vincent had no feeling of rebellion. Although he was now thirty-two years old, he still was not ready to stand on his own feet. And there would be one great advantage about this new location. He would be living directly across the river from Pierre's Oratory. But he would not go running with every small problem. Aside from the hours he must spend in the schoolroom, he would keep to his own little cell, occupying himself with prayer and meditation. God would solve the problems.

The immediate problems were the boys themselves. Bold and boisterous, interested in nothing but sports and mischief, they put in their time sullenly. From the very beginning, Vincent knew he would accomplish little with them. When Madame de Gondi took to sitting in on the lessons, he considered it an indication that she was not satisfied with the results he was getting with her mutinous young sons.

"They are learning very little, Madame", Vincent said one day after the two had wrestled themselves out of the room. "Perhaps I am not a good teacher. If you wish to find someone else . . ."

He paused, for the pretty lady had turned white as the lace of her ruff.

"Oh, Monsieur, you wouldn't leave us! Tell me you wouldn't!" she begged, and to his horror she seemed about to fall on her knees before him.

Vincent murmured something and turned to go. He

had seen some of Madame's tantrums. Deeply religious, sweet, of a generally lovable character, nevertheless she had a childish streak in her of demanding her own way. Her husband, the dashing and handsome general, would laugh and tease and finally give in to her. But Vincent had no intention of humoring her. He would remain a little while longer. Then, if the boys showed no improvement, he would tell de Bérulle he must leave.

"Monsieur, I have been thinking of how much there is to do here", Madame said quickly, to keep him in the room.

Vincent paused politely. "There is almost nothing, Madame. Your sons could learn as much and more from someone else. Your household attends Mass daily, and so there is no need for me to exhort them to goodness. And you and your husband, Madame, are examples of Christian living."

"But what of the people on our estates, the sick, the newborn babies who may die without baptism, the widows and the orphans who need us? Don't you want to help them, Monsieur?"

Vincent looked at the beautiful taffeta gown, the dainty hands unsoiled by work. "You already give generous alms, Madame. No one starves on your estates. And the parish priests attend to the marrying, burying, and baptizing."

"There are few priests, sir, who take their duties seriously. You would be far more likely to find them in a ballroom than at the bedside of a dying peasant."

The First Mission

Madame was right, of course, but Vincent was surprised that she should remark such a thing. Her small chin was set now in determination. She had something in mind about which she intended to get her own way.

"Would you make a short trip with me out through the estates, Monsieur? Only good would be bound to come of it! Will you do it?"

"As you wish, Madame."

With that consent, a new era began for Vincent, one that would end only when he tottered for the last time into his little cell and sat down in his chair to die. On horseback beside the carriage, he rode over the vast estates, to Folleville and Clichy and all the villages. Conditions were far worse than Madame had suggested. There was work here for more than one man's lifetime.

Madame de Gondi laid off her taffeta for a dress of plain wool. Then she went from one hut to another, teaching and nursing, with Vincent following her to administer the sacraments. By the end of the year, the de Gondi estates had become famous for their physical and spiritual well-being. Madame, taking the shortest time possible away from her duties to give birth to another son, requested that Vincent become her spiritual director. Her present confessor, she said, was so ignorant that he did not even know the words of absolution. Vincent did not wish to be so closely associated with this woman, who could be so demanding at times. But at de Bérulle's request, he gave in. Madame became completely dedicated to her charitable work, and through her the field would widen for Vincent.

On a December night in 1616, Vincent was called to the bedside of a dying peasant. He knew the man and knew he had gone regularly to Mass and the sacraments, yet for some reason he felt he should ask for a general confession. The man refused. Vincent, alarmed and puzzled, dispatched a boy to bring Madame de Gondi, for her gift for getting what she wanted had often been put to good use. Kneeling on the dirt floor, she begged the man to make a good confession. Like other men, he gave in to Madame.

Afterward, weeping, he called her back into the room.

"You have saved my soul from hell, Madame! I lived outwardly as a good Catholic, but I had mortal sins on my soul, and I was too ashamed of them to confess them! Now you have brought me peace!"

The family, hearing the weeping, crowded into the room. The daughter burst into tears, kissed the hem of Vincent's cassock, and asked that he hear her confession also. In the next hour each member of the family made a general confession, and their grief over their father's illness turned to devout thankfulness. Vincent was so moved he was near to tears himself. Even at Clichy he had seen nothing like the spiritual uplift of these poor people. What should it mean to him?

As so often happened, Madame had the answer. Vincent must preach a sermon the next Sunday on the great good to be gained by general confession. Folleville, it seemed, would be the best place, within reach of the most people. She would send messengers throughout the estates to spread the word. Vincent agreed readily and prepared a sermon with great care.

Sunday, January 25, 1617, was a chilly day with snow blowing lightly along the ground, but the cold did not keep the peasants at home. They packed into the little church until there was no more room, and the latecomers had to stand outside. But they all heard the sermon. Vincent knew from the way they listened that he would have a good response, but he did not expect the landslide that came. Every person in the church remained to go to confession. By late afternoon, when Vincent paused for the bowl of soup Madame insisted he take, the waiting line stretched through the cemetery clear to the creek.

"They are going home and sending others!" Madame exclaimed. "But you can't hear them all. I'll send to Amiens for some Jesuits to help."

The Jesuits came, gasped at the numbers of penitents, and went to work with Vincent. Nothing like it had ever been known before.

The miracle of Folleville became the talk of the day. Pastors of some of the great churches of Paris invited Vincent to preach in their pulpits; praise flowed around him; Madame treated him with reverence. Twenty-five years later, Vincent would commemorate the twenty-fifth of January as the beginning of his immense work of the missions. But at the time, he was tortured. Praise might inspire pride. Glory was obnoxious, and yet the fame of his sermons was bringing a host of lost souls back to the Church.

In his distress he slipped across the river to talk with his friend de Bérulle.

"I'm afraid, Pierre", he confessed. "Terribly afraid!"

"Of what? Our Lord became famous for his sermons. It didn't bother him."

Vincent laughed for the first time in a week. "I know. If I touch people's hearts, it is because the Lord gave me the gift, and he will give me the humility that must go with it."

"Well, if you understand all that, what are you afraid of?"

"Of Madame de Gondi, really. She has put me on a pedestal where I don't fit at all. I hate it!"

Pierre smiled. "Poor Madame!" Then he said briskly, "Vincent, how would you like to go to Chatillon of the Lakes, down in Bresse? It's several days' ride from here."

"Anything, Pierre! When can I go?"

"You may not thank me when you see it."

"Madame will argue against my going. And I'll give in to her!"

"Then we won't tell her", Pierre said practically. "Let her think you're going to Clichy. Where is the general?"

"Down at Marseilles with the galleys."

"There you are! Write him a letter from Chatillon."

"Madame has been good to me. It hardly seems right."

Pierre put his arm across Vincent's shoulders. "My friend, Madame is a holy woman, but she is also a holy terror when she doesn't get what she wants. Right now she wants you, but she doesn't need you any more. Another priest can very well take your place. Now go in peace!"

Vincent went. Never in his life had he felt more relieved than when he mounted his horse and left the House of Gondi behind him.

He knew nothing about Chatillon of the Lakes. As he rode through streets lined with taverns from which came sounds of revelry and boarded-up houses from which came no sounds at all, he couldn't help wondering what sort of place this was that Pierre had chosen for him. He halted his horse before the church. The door sagged open. The windows were broken. The only human being in sight was a rather tipsy young man coming singing down the muddy street. Seeing Vincent, he gave an uncertain salute.

"A priest, eh? I haven't seen a cassock in years." He waved toward the church. "Walk in, Father. The pigeons won't mind. Nobody will. You'll have no congregation here."

"There must be a few Catholics in the town",

Vincent said quietly. "Some nobleman built a chapel here, and there are six chantry priests."

The young man folded his arms around the hitching post. "You know, you're right. But all the chantry priests do is sing for the nobleman's soul, as they've been endowed to do, and go to parties. Everybody's a Calvinist, like me. Always fighting."

"Is that why you live in boarded-up houses?"

"Maybe. Where are you going to stay tonight, Father?"

"Isn't there a house for the pastor?"

"Oh, yes. But you'll have to chase Eleanor's pig out first. You better come home with me, Father. John Beynier, that's me. Come on."

For a few days, until he could make his own house habitable, Vincent rented lodgings from John. It was through him that he learned of the odd state of affairs in the town. The Protestant Huguenots lived in the houses that had been barricades during the days of war. Now the barricades were of use against the highwaymen and criminals with which the town was infested, but since many of the townspeople gave shelter to these ruffians for a good price, the constables made no effort to run them out. At the edge of town, on a huge estate, lived a nobleman, Balthazar de Rougemont, baron of Chandes. He was a bully, extremely wealthy, and a famous duellist. Around him there had gathered a carefree society. On the fringe of everything, treated as if they were not there, lived a miserable scattering of poor peasants who made no attempt to attend Mass.

As he had done at Clichy, Vincent enlisted some of the peasant women to clean the church. Before noon, the husbands peered around the broken door, caught the cheery talk of this priest who had pinned up his cassock and was working right with the women, and hurried home for hammer and nails. The next day a doctor of

The First Mission

theology came out from Lyons in response to Vincent's request for an assistant, and by the following Sunday the two priests were installed in their own house, and the church was ready for the congregation.

A small crowd, mostly peasants, came to Mass. In the back were a few stylishly dressed ladies. When they began to chatter behind their fans, Vincent turned, fastened his eyes upon them, and waited until they were quiet. Then he went on with his Mass, and the ladies did not offend again. He gave the same sermon that had struck such fire in Folleville. The results were such that he and the doctor of theology were hearing confessions far into the night.

The local magistrate, after a talk with Vincent, agreed to enforce the law against the harboring of criminals. The six chantry priests stopped going to social functions and began wearing their cassocks. Religion became so fashionable that the church was crowded for daily Mass. The swashbuckling baron came one Sunday out of curiosity. His conversion was as violent as his former life had been. After a few conferences with Vincent he was completely won over. He sold all his possessions, keeping only his sword.

"But that too must go", he said sadly to Vincent. "I have loved it beyond anything in the world, but now it ties me to the world. I must be free to follow the will of God!"

And he dashed the fine blade to pieces against a rock.

Not every edifying incident in Chatillon was as spectacular as the baron's conversion. The development that was to have its greatest bearing upon Vincent's future grew out of a simple beginning. A poor family living a mile or so out of town was on the verge of starvation. In his Sunday sermon, Vincent mentioned the family's need. That evening he took a walk out along the road to the peasant's farm and met crowds of people returning from the farm. Not merely the wealthy had sent alms, but those who had only a few loaves of bread had divided with the starving family. At the farm there was such a store of provisions as would feed many families. Much of it was perishable. Some would go to waste, and the unfortunate ones would be hungry again.

Vincent paced his floor long that night, working out the problem. There must be some kind of organization, he decided, to handle such situations. Many peasant families were in want. If supplies could be gathered at a central point and portioned out, everyone could eat, and nothing would be wasted.

"Your plan is a very good one", said the doctor of theology. "A charitable confraternity of some kind would solve the problem. But it is a big undertaking to procure the goods and deal them out fairly. You have no money to pay for such services. Who would do this for you?"

"John Beynier", Vincent said promptly.

"Our young Calvinist?"

"Our devout young Catholic. His reformation is the despair of his hoodlum friends. John will do it."

Thus the first Confraternity of Charity came into being. In the years to come, Vincent's confraternities would serve the whole of France, the answer to poverty in peacetime and the salvation of the country in time of war.

With the wide scope of work now opening before him, Vincent was happy. There was only one irritation. Madame de Gondi, finally advised by her husband that Vincent was gone for good, was in a panic. For days she had wept, unable to eat or sleep. She had written long letters to Vincent, at first pleading, then threatening that if he did not return she would hold him responsible for all that might happen to her. Vincent paid no heed to the first letters beyond making one reply. But by late autumn he was afraid Madame was winning. She was appealing to every friend she had in Paris, and they were many. Finally, to settle the matter, Vincent agreed to consult the superior of the Oratory at Lyons. That cautious father would make no decision.

"You should take this up with Pierre de Bérulle", he urged. "He is your friend and my superior. He will know."

Vincent rode slowly back to Chatillon. Pierre would side with Madame, for she had the support of the archbishop of Paris, who was her brother-in-law and who never argued with her, and Pierre would of course agree with the archbishop.

So Vincent gave away his possessions as he had done at Clichy, and once again he set out for Paris. The people of Chatillon came near to staging a riot when he left.

As he rode north, it seemed to Vincent that every step was tearing him farther away from his vow to serve the poor. He said as much to de Bérulle the instant they met.

"I don't honestly think so, Vincent", Pierre said. "Oh, I agree I am influenced by the archbishop, but I'd never let him sway me to something I felt was wrong. No, I believe you have finished in Chatillon. That work will go on without you."

"You said the same when I left Madame de Gondi," Vincent reminded him, "yet now you would send me back."

"I know, but not to do the same work. Paris is the heart of the kingdom. From here, all of France will be your parish. I would never advise you to come back merely for the good of Madame de Gondi, although she may think so. But she will not dominate you as she did before. And for the real extension of your work, Vincent, this is the place!"

On Christmas Eve of 1617, within the same year he had departed, Vincent rode back across the Seine to the House of Gondi. He couldn't help feeling that once again Madame had had her way. In spite of Pierre's assurance, it would take a little time for him to see that Madame's way was also God's way.

5

THE TIME TO RUN

As Pierre de Bérulle had promised, Vincent's return to the House of Gondi was not a return to the old life. He would be spiritual director to Madame, and he would oversee the education of the boys, but a tutor took his place in the schoolroom, and Vincent was left free to travel and work wherever he chose in the estates. His absence from Paris, far from making people forget him, had only added to his fame, for everyone had chattered for months about his mysterious disappearance.

Now that he was back, Madame de Gondi was joyfully spreading the news of what he had done in Chatillon. He could not silence her.

But when he undertook to establish a confraternity in Folleville, he found that all the talk about Chatillon was of value. The people flocked to the church throughout the mission that he preached, then rushed to carry out his plans. In a short time nearly thirty confraternities were established throughout the estates, and the relief of the poor became the fashionable thing. The organizations were very simple. In each community ladies of the upper class who would have the means and the time were drawn together into a society, and officers elected. Then they were carefully instructed by Vincent.

"You must see the person of Christ in the sick", he would tell them at their first meeting. "If the place is filthy, clean it. If the patient is rude, smile at him. Many of the peasants will be downright mean when you try to help them, and you will hear low language and see things that will sicken you. But remember always, what you do unto the least of these, you do unto Christ himself, and if he makes the doing hard for you, then think how much greater is the service you give him!"

The women responded with such alacrity that Vincent was dumbfounded. The husbands complained only mildly when their wives demanded large amounts for alms. This Vincent, they smiled to one another, was an expensive fad, and their pretty creatures would soon be diverted to something else.

But the diversion did not come. Hard though the women worked, the charities outgrew their efforts, and at Folleville, in 1620, Vincent de Paul founded his first organization of men. The brotherhood took over the administration of funds, while the women cared for the aged and the sick. Soon this movement also spread. Vincent's only fear was that the vastness of his undertakings might be their downfall. But as time went by and the work only grew more solid and dependable, even he was satisfied.

"I started with nothing in mind but the relief of one poor family at Chatillon", Vincent said one day to Madame de Gondi. "The movement has grown by itself. All I ask of God is, what next?"

Madame thought this over carefully. Since her son Henry had been killed in a fall from a horse, she had been more dedicated to her charities than ever before.

"I have been wondering about the beggars", she said. "The king drives them out of Paris by law every once in a while, but they flock back again. If we could accept the fact that we must have them and then *do* something about them, wouldn't it be better?"

"It would, indeed. I believe we will put them to work, Madame."

"Doing what, Monsieur? They are so ignorant!"

"We'll give them shovels and let them dig a ditch and pay them a small wage. Earning is an improvement over begging!"

A few days later people passing the old saltpeter works

saw a hundred or so men busily digging a ditch through the marsh, the newest of Monsieur Vincent's projects. It was a revolutionary idea, that the beggars might have self-respect restored to them through earning a living. A week after the digging began, the men began filling in the dirt again because Monsieur Vincent had not needed the ditch in the first place. It was the men who needed the work.

"What will he think of next?" people wondered, and once more the peasant priest was the talk of Paris.

Anyone might stop Vincent on the street to talk, for to him no one was a stranger. He was not surprised, then, when a poor woman spoke to him one day.

"Father, save my son! He was with the thieves when the king's archers caught them, but he is not a thief! He got in with bad company! They can't send him to the galleys!"

Patiently, Vincent listened to her story. He had thought of visiting the prisons, but it was never his way to seek out new work. It must come to him. Let God do the seeking. Perhaps God was ready now. And so, unquestioning, Vincent tramped out along the street of Saint Anthony to the Bastille.

"Musset?" the keeper answered his query through the bars. "I have no list of names. I don't know who is here."

"He was brought in yesterday", said Vincent, "from the magistrate's court. Surely you know which ones came yesterday. Take me to them, please."

The keeper made a large rattle of unlocking the door. "Well, it's your stomach, Father", he said, and taking a lighted torch he led the way into a black corridor. From either side through barred slits came the moaning of men and the clank of chains. The man paid no attention.

"The last ones were put in here", he said, pausing before one of the black pockets. "You, Musset, are you there?"

"What do you want with me?" a young voice demanded from the dark.

"Now what, Father?" the keeper asked.

"Open the door. Let me go in."

"Well, keep to the middle of the floor, then, so they can't reach you."

He loosened the heavy bars, and Vincent stepped inside. This was an underground dungeon, and there was no light except from the torch. Around the walls, blinking in the unaccustomed glare, men were chained. The chains were too short for them to lie down, and some of them half hung, asleep. The length of their stay could be judged from the length of their beards. A young man with only a dark stubble lunged the short space of his chain.

"Father, get me out of here!" he cried. "I'm innocent. I swear I'm innocent!"

The man beside him had a beard hanging to his waist. "I was innocent, too. This rotten prison is full of innocent men!"

Vincent walked slowly forward over the moldy straw.

The chained creatures peered at him more like animals than men. He spread out his hands as if he would embrace them all and spoke softly.

"My friends, my children! God bless you!"

Silence fell. It might have been the first time some of them had heard the name of God spoken as anything but a curse. Vincent walked around the circle, pressing the hand of each prisoner, talking gently. The men watched him with suspicion. In the shabby cassock and coarse thick shoes, he was not in the class of the noblemen who came slumming as the climax to a night of revelry. But distrust and hatred had been built up through bitter years, and Vincent did not expect to win confidence in a minute. Sitting down on a large stone, he took the crucifix from his belt and held it up.

"There is a Man who really was innocent," he said, "but look at the suffering he went through. For you and me. Because he loved us."

"You, maybe," a man grumbled, "but there's nothing to love about us!"

"Your suffering, as great as his own. I have none to offer him."

"Let me see that!"

The keeper made a movement of restraint, but Vincent walked over and laid the crucifix in the filthy hand. Then again he went to each man, letting him hold the cross while he spoke of what it meant.

"Now I must go," he said at last, "but I'll be here tomorrow with a basket of food. And I'll bring paper and write down all the messages you would like to have sent to your families."

Several of the men began to weep. Vincent lifted his hand in blessing.

"Father, I was one of them. I'm guilty!" young Musset choked. "But don't tell my mother! Let her believe I'm her good son!"

Leaving the prison, Vincent went first to the magistrate in the Palace of Justice to inquire about the length of the sentence given young Musset. The magistrate made indefinite noises, searched through records, and finally gave the answer he had known from the beginning.

"It is not set down. When he has served long enough, he will be let go."

"And who decides when a man has served long enough?" Vincent demanded. "Monsieur de Gondi?"

"Sir, de Gondi is the commander! No, perhaps the galley sergeant. I don't know." The magistrate's face had grown very red, and he sputtered. "There are never enough rowers for the galleys, sir! If a man's sentence is prolonged a year or two, what's the difference? He's doing his patriotic duty in the service of the king!"

Vincent turned on his heel. His humility never permitted him to become indignant over injustice to himself, but the torment of these friendless, forgotten men cried to heaven for a defender. In the beautiful house that was his home now, Vincent went straight to Phillippe-Emmanuel de Gondi himself. Simply, he described the dungeons, then went on to his visit with the magistrate.

"I am sure you knew little or nothing of this, sir", he finished. "We realize men are condemned to the galleys, we see them pass on the road to Bordeaux or Marseilles and leave behind them a few dead, but we do not think of them as human beings with immortal souls. They are wrongdoers, they deserve punishment, but must they be sent to hell by you, sir?"

"By me? I did not condemn them!"

"But you are their master on earth, and you are responsible to God for their immortal souls!"

"Bless me, what a thought! What do you want me to do?"

"Speak to the king about having the records properly kept. Then, sir, give me permission as your almoner to help these abandoned men."

"Oh, by all means, go right ahead!" the general agreed, and it was evident from his manner that he had half expected Vincent to demand his personal attention for this new undertaking.

Vincent secured a large house and had it thoroughly cleaned and furnished like a hospital. Then, in a great procession that astounded Paris, the men were taken out of the dungeons and under heavy guard transferred to the house. People thronged the streets and surrounded the house, thrilled and excited. Money was offered before Vincent asked for it. Conversions and returns to the faith among the criminals were so numerous that Vincent could not count them.

On February 8, 1619, Louis XIII signed royal letters

of patent making Vincent the royal almoner. The stipend of his office was six hundred livres a year, more than a living for him. All other royal almoners were to be under him. Vincent shrank from the honor, but he was delighted with his new powers. Not only were the convict prisons of the entire kingdom under his care, but he could visit the galleys when they lay in port and minister to the men. Immediately he planned a tour that would touch every port and prison.

"I don't know where this new duty will lead me," he said to Madame de Gondi upon his departure, "but where God wills me to go, I will go. We must not tread on the heels of Providence, but when God opens the way, run! And now is the time to run."

Vincent left Paris with a group of prisoners bound for Le Havre, nearly 150 miles to the northwest. Marching with them by day, sleeping in whatever stable they were sheltered in at night, he encouraged them to obedience and patience. Their crimes were never mentioned. When they reached Le Havre and saw the galleys lying at anchor, a groan went up from the men.

"The galleys are better than prison", Vincent told them. "You will be out in the sun and air; you will be given better food and clean water to drink. And who but you would have the strength to handle a sixty-foot oar with only five men to an oar?"

In silence the men filed to their places, five on a bench, until the fifty benches were filled. Each man had only eighteen inches of space. Here, with his left foot chained to the footboard, he would remain even to sleep until the ship touched shore again. But aboard each of the galleys now there would be a priest who must answer to Vincent for his spiritual care of the convicts.

Raising his hand in blessing, Vincent said good-bye to these men he had come to love as if they were children and went ashore. The whip would still sting, and the muscles would throb with fatigue, but the men were not despairing. Monsieur Vincent was their friend. He had assured them there would be an end to their sentences, and they were proud of the great offering they could make to God.

Through the summer Vincent went on to Calais and Dunkirk and Marseilles, ending his long tour at Bordeaux. Now he was free to return to Paris. But Bordeaux was only seventy-five miles from Pouy, and he had not seen his home since he left twenty-four years ago with the oxen money in his pocket. Now, having even less, attired in a cassock through which his elbows had finally poked, in the heavy shoes and battered hat he had worn through the rains of summer, he started out on foot for Pouy. The road ran along the seacoast, and when the sun was warm he took off his shoes to walk in the sand. That was how he arrived in Pouy, his shoes in his hand. The first people he met passed him up as a beggar.

Nothing had changed about the old place. John's children played in the dooryard; the old mother came out to see why the dog was barking and could hardly believe her eyes when she saw Vincent. His ambition had been to do a great deal for his family. Now he saw that his best gift would be to give them nothing. They were humble people, born to a poor station in life, and there they were content. This would be his last visit to them. He must break all earthly ties to free himself for his work.

For several days Vincent remained in Pouy. When he left, tramping away on foot, his vision was so blurred with tears that he could not see the road. God in his own good time would take from him this attachment for his family, but the long journey back to Paris was filled with wretchedness. At home with the de Gondis, he plunged so hard into his work that Madame scolded him for his complete disregard of his health.

"You must delegate some of the work to others", she insisted. "Get a company of priests together to help you. The money I put aside long ago for such a foundation is still there."

Vincent rose from the small table where he had been working. Madame never entered his room but would come often, as she had done now, for a conference from the doorway.

"You know how I have requested priests from the Jesuits and the Oratorians, Madame", Vincent reminded her. "They have none to spare."

"Then start your own company, Monsieur. Oh, I know you feel you are not the one to direct them. But you will come to realize as I do that only you can train and oversee the priests who will carry on your work of the missions!"

Vincent smiled humbly. So often Madame was right. She had suggested the sermon at Folleville, the start of all the missions. Could she be right about the mission foundation? Was he holding back because actually he did not want assistance? Was he again being the boy who nearly refused the oxen money because he wished to have all the glory of accomplishment for himself?

"Monsieur Vincent, are you ill?" Madame asked, in her concern stepping across the threshold. "Do sit down! You look terrible!"

"I am not ill, Madame, no. It is the matter of the company."

"Then you will start it, Monsieur? Really?"

Vincent held up his hand as if he would barricade himself from Madame's enthusiasm. "I must think about it and pray a great deal. It would be a tremendous responsibility, and I'm not at all sure that I'm either worthy or capable."

"God knows you are worthy of responsibility, Monsieur. And so do I!"

But still Vincent shook his head. The shivering was taking hold of him now. "I would need young priests, because the older ones would not agree with my methods. And young priests must have a school, and where would we obtain a suitable building?"

"My husband", Madame said promptly. "He will know exactly how to go about everything."

"He is already building a hospital for the galley slaves at Bordeaux", Vincent reminded her gently. "Perhaps that is enough."

"I will decide what is enough", she said. "Once again, Monsieur, it is the time to run!"

When she had gone, Vincent seated himself again at the table. Madame's health, always delicate, was becoming a great concern to her husband, and he never denied her slightest wish. The building was as good as here. Vincent drew a piece of paper toward him. He must make a retreat in order to be certain that he was not mistaking personal ambition for the will of God. But at the top of the paper he wrote the name of Anthony Portail. Young Anthony had been of the most heart-warming assistance with the galley slaves. He would be the first of the mission priests—if the time had come to run.

6

LOUISE

IN THAT YEAR of 1625, which was to mark so great a change in his life, Vincent de Paul was forty-four years old. Already, with his confraternities, his work among the beggars, and his office as royal almoner, he had accomplished enough for one man's lifetime. But now his enormous service was about to begin. Madame de Gondi, true to her word, had gone immediately to her husband about the matter of housing for Vincent's company of priests, and de Gondi had gone to his brother, the archbishop of Paris. The archbishop had the answer. The old School of the Good Children on the south bank of the Seine, built in the thirteenth century, was battered and timeworn but still in use as a school for a handful of indifferent students. The archbishop appointed Vincent the principal of the school. He could take whomever he wished as students.

On April 17, the papers were signed that were to be the contract for the new congregation. The services of the missionaries were to be confined to the country and small villages. No fee ever would be taken. Expenses would be paid from a travel fund held in common. Spiritual care of the poor was to be their only duty. The company were to be bound by vows and yet live as seculars. For this reason, because Vincent appeared to be establishing a religious order and yet was not, approval was long in coming from the Vatican.

The only real hindrance, however, was the one laid down by Madame de Gondi herself. The new company could function while the Holy Father wondered whether or not to approve it; but with its superior required to live in the House of Gondi instead of at the School of the Good Children, administration would be awkward.

But God, wishing to be served, removed the restriction in his own way. Barely two months after the signing of the agreement, on June 25, Madame de Gondi died. She had burned out her fragile strength in her works of charity. Her final request was that Vincent remain with her family for the rest of his life.

De Gondi was far away in Marseilles when Madame took sick, and there was no time to send for him. Vincent could not write such news in a letter. Leaving Anthony Portail at the school, he journeyed to Marseilles. The general was stricken by the loss of his beloved wife. Even in his grief, however, he could see the absurdity of requiring Vincent to remain with his sons, and he released him from the promise. Two years later de Gondi resigned his post, disposed of his wealth, and entered the Oratory, where for thirty-four years he lived the humble life of a brother.

At last Vincent was completely free. Within two weeks he had returned to Paris and moved into the school, but Anthony was his only companion. A third priest was necessary to begin the missions, for Anthony was still too shy to give a sermon.

Vincent, praying continually for another priest, made a visit one day to the old church of Saint Nicholas of the Coins. The only other person in the church was a woman, heavily veiled in black, weeping as if her heart would break. Vincent was moved with compassion and spoke to her.

"Someone has died, Madame?"

"Not yet, Father. But my husband is dying."

"It is God's will. Pray for his eternal rest."

"I'm not afraid for him, Monsieur. He will go to heaven. But I'm afraid for myself! I have offended God terribly, and this is my punishment!"

She poured out her fears to Vincent. Upon the death

of her father when she was fourteen, she had made a vow that she would never marry but would enter a convent. Her spiritual adviser, believing she was not meant for the convent, had dispensed young Louise de Marillac from her vow and seen her married to a suitable husband, Anthony le Gras, secretary to Marie de' Medici.

"But God is angry with me for breaking my vow", she ended. "I cannot get away from his wrath!"

"Your confessor released you from your vow, a perfectly right thing to do", Vincent told her quietly. "When you are free, come and see me at the School of the Good Children. In the meantime, let your mind be at rest."

Vincent forgot about Louise de Marillac, for his prayers were answered by the arrival of Francis du Coudray, a doctor of the Sorbonne University, and he could set out on his first mission. Leaving the house key with a neighbor, Vincent, Anthony Portail, and the new priest started out on foot. Eating as little as they could, for funds were low, sleeping on the ground at night if they happened to be traveling, they made a long round of missions. In strange parishes they were often taken for beggars. With a good escort of dogs and children, they would go first to the pastor to ask permission to conduct a mission in his church, and the request was never refused. Returning to the marketplace, the three would talk with the people, asking about their work and their crops and their families. When a small crowd had gathered, Vincent, his eyes twinkling, would address them all.

"So, my friends, you wonder who we are, where we

have come from, and most of all you wonder what we want from you. Nothing. Listen now, and I will tell you about us."

Smiling, joking sometimes, Vincent would chat until the crowd was laughing with him. Then, speaking in the daily language of his listeners, moving often among the people and talking straight to them, he used his "Little Method" to explain the goodness of virtue, what virtue is, and how to go about attaining it in their daily lives. Over and over as they tramped the country roads, Vincent and his companions had thought through their sermons so that when the time came to preach they could speak naturally. The method worked so beautifully that no one could believe it was planned. This was, the pastors said, just Vincent's way, which he had taught to his companions.

At Christmas the missionaries returned to Paris for a brief rest. On Christmas Day Vincent had a visitor, a small shivering woman in black who sat on one of the two chairs in the unheated room, her hands clinging together in cold and nervousness.

"God took him yesterday, sir", Louise de Marillac said. "What am I to do now with my life? I am drowned in a sea of doubt!"

Vincent looked at the lips drawn together to keep from trembling, at the eyes that held such torment. Mademoiselle de Marillac, as she was called in accord with the custom of that time, had great spiritual power, but she was concerned only with herself.

"Time must give you the answer, Mademoiselle", he said gently. "We can't rush God. He had his own Son wait thirty years before beginning his teaching."

The thin hands flew up. "I can't wait years, Monsieur! I must know!"

"Let me think about it", Vincent said, and that was the only answer he would give.

Soon after Christmas the missionaries again locked up their house, handed the key to the obliging neighbor, and trudged away on foot. Each time they returned, Louise de Marillac was there to beg Vincent to tell her what to do. Her misgivings over her broken vow, her alarm at the conduct of her spoiled thirteen-year-old son, her overzealousness in prayer—all these anxieties, told over and over, finally tried Vincent's patience.

"Mademoiselle, there are many people worse off than you!" he told her one day. "Think of someone other than yourself—the beggars, for instance, the sick lying alone and uncared for. When you look at your son who has too much, think of the foundlings who are abandoned in the streets. *Think*, Mademoiselle!"

It was a strong speech for Vincent. Ashamed, Louise went away. When he returned from his next mission journey, he was astounded by the change in her. She was completely calm, and she smiled for the first time.

"I did think, sir", she told him quietly. "I realized my own selfishness. So I sold my big house, and I sent my son away to the Jesuits. I live now only a few doors from here, and I fill my days with work for the poor." She paused, again smiling. "Through you, Monsieur, I am going to give my life to the poor. Tell me what to do, and I will do it."

Vincent was silent, thinking of how God had put him also through a time of torment, and peace had come only when he vowed to give his life to the poor. Louise's experience had been so similar that it seemed God must be sending her to aid in this great work of charity.

"Go on as you are, Mademoiselle", he said at last. "I can give you no better guidance than your own heart has already given you. Perhaps in time God will reveal more of his divine plan to us."

The plan soon became apparent. The confraternities needed a central authority for the more even distribution of supplies. Herds of sheep and cattle in the country could help feed and clothe the poor of the cities, and money would be kept in a general treasury for all. Louise would be the administrator. Her own personal fortune was ample for her own expenses and her son's at school. She would be carrying out her vow of service to the poor and at the same time making use of her talents for organization.

Vincent had expected her to take up the task with enthusiasm, but her zeal surprised even him. Immediately, in her own plain coach, she departed on a tour of all the confraternities, stopping at each long enough to become familiar with the people and their problems. Reports of her doings filtered back to Vincent. With marvelous tact she was binding together an organization.

He could trace her path through the country by the requests coming in for new confraternities. Daily he thanked God for Louise.

Back again in Paris, Mademoiselle de Marillac plunged eagerly into the planning of charities in the city parishes. Vincent had founded only one city confraternity because there the poor were supposedly cared for through the king's bounty. Louise used her friendships to assemble the court ladies into charitable work. There was one difficulty. The titled ladies would not associate with anyone of lower rank, and so these confraternities became exclusive little social circles.

"Let them have it their way", Vincent told Louise with a twinkle in his eye. "*All* their way. When there is food to be cooked for the sick, cleaning to be done, let them do it themselves. Unless they learn the satisfaction of working with the hands, the novelty will wear off, and the charities will be left in your lap."

So for a time the Ladies of Charity cooked and scrubbed and ministered to the sick, but by the end of the year fewer of them bustled into Louise's house, and a growing number of serving maids came and went.

"The maids do the work even better than the ladies," Louise told Vincent, "but they serve because it is their duty, and they want to get through in a hurry. The kindness to the sick is missing. I try to tell them that they are serving Christ in these poor people, and they answer politely enough, but the looks they give me, Monsieur! I don't know what to do about it!"

"Perhaps I do, Mademoiselle", Vincent said and sat down to write a letter.

A week or so later, the first of Louise's helpers arrived. She was a peasant girl named Margaret Naseau, a member of the confraternity at Suresnes. Like all country girls of the time, she never had gone to school. Painfully saving a few sous, she had bought an alphabet and asked the parish priest to teach her the letters. Then, following her sheep out on the hills, she had taught herself to read. As soon as she knew one letter from another, she gathered the children and began her teaching. By the time Vincent asked her to come to Paris, the older girls whom she had taught were able to take over her little school. She was still only seventeen when she joined Louise.

"You should see her, sir, working with the ladies!" Louise told Vincent joyfully. "Rank means nothing to her. And with the sick she is an angel! If only you could find more like her for me, Monsieur!"

There were no more exactly like Margaret, but other girls from the provinces joined Louise and became devoted workers. The ladies, instead of losing interest, became more diligent. Soon France would have need of every means of relief for suffering, for the terrible war that would reduce the country to despair was already stirring. Louise's two uncles were imprisoned. Louise was too busy to fall into her former despondency, for Paris was jammed with people whose homes had been despoiled by the soldiers and who now flocked to the city to be fed.

Vincent, in the old School of the Good Children, saw his community growing beyond capacity. God must soon find his Company a bigger place. But he was not thinking of his immediate needs when he received the fat monk who was the prior of the Augustinians out in the enormous old leper house called Saint-Lazare.

"I am in charge of a fine congregation", the prior said rather pompously. "Saint-Lazare dates from the twelfth century. We still hold the old feudal rights of high, middle, and low jurisdiction; we have our own sheriff and court of justice and of course prisons. Inside our enclosure, which is the largest in Paris, we have our own gardens, stables, slaughterhouse—everything to make us a separate little city."

The monk paused to glance around the bare little room as if he did not think much of it. Then he resumed.

"Saint-Lazare is a tradition, sir. When a king is crowned, he comes there to receive the oaths of allegiance from all the tradesmen. And when he dies, the funeral procession pauses there for the blessing of the monks before going on its way to Saint-Denis for burial. We hold the respect of Paris, sir!" His voice dropped. "And all of this, naturally, brings in a large revenue."

Again he paused, and Vincent murmured, "Indeed, you seem to have no problems, sir."

"Oh, but I do! The revenue does not nearly keep up the place—in fact, some of the buildings are falling down. But that is not my greatest concern, sir." He leaned forward confidentially, and the old chair creaked. "Actually, I can no longer discipline my priests. They have grown lax, indolent, disrespectful—the situation is intolerable!"

"And you wish me to suggest a remedy, sir?"

"I wish you to move in—to take over Saint-Lazare!"

Vincent stared at Adrian le Bon. He could not have heard right. "I could not take on the administration of another order, sir. Already I am superior of the Order of the Visitation because Francis de Sales insisted upon it. And I have my own Company of the Mission."

"That's the whole idea, Vincent! Move your priests in with my monks; let them live in the same dormitories, eat at the same tables, say Mass at the same altars, and within a year I'll have a different congregation."

Vincent clasped his hands firmly around the crucifix at his belt. Surely it was the devil, not God, who sent this monk to him. To take over Saint-Lazare would be a direct violation of his vow of poverty.

"Are you ill, Monsieur?" the prior asked, and he jumped up in alarm. The ancient floor shook under him. "You are trembling! Shall I call someone?"

Slowly Vincent arose from his chair. Fixing his gaze firmly but respectfully on the prior, he replied.

"We are a humble community, sir. We practice poverty in the service of the poor. We could never live in so fine a place as Saint-Lazare."

"But I tell you, sir, that's just the point! The place is no longer fine; it is falling to pieces! You can live in as abject poverty as you like, personally, for you will find it no trouble at all to put every sou into maintenance."

"The prestige of living at Saint-Lazare would not befit us, sir."

"Well, then, think of the good influence your priests would be on mine!"

"Do you keep the rule of silence, Prior le Bon?"

"No—no, I can't say that we do. Rather difficult to enforce, isn't it?"

Vincent smiled. "We do not enforce our rules, sir. We keep them because that is our way of life. But it could be upset, I'm afraid. Instead of your monks being silent, my priests might take to chattering like magpies."

"We could work out something—"

"No, sir", Vincent said with solid firmness. "Thank you for your offer, but we must decline. Perhaps someone else will take it."

"You'll change your mind", the prior declared. "Why, this old place is bulging with all it contains!"

"That is only too true, sir."

"If your Company is growing the way I hear, you'll soon be glad of a priory to put them in. I'll be back in six months."

Undisturbed, Vincent bade good day to the monk. He did not mention the conversation to any of his Company, yet somehow the news leaked out. Monsieur Vincent had turned down the fine property of Saint-Lazare! Vincent heard the whispers and paid no attention. Only one thought bothered him. Passing along the road to Saint-Denis, he had heard the wild lamentings of the insane who were housed in small huts in the garden of Saint-Lazare. Perhaps, if he had taken the prior's offer, he might he able to do something for the poor things. There was no cure for insanity, but kindness might help a little. With the ending of the Crusades, leprosy had almost died out, and there was no use any more for Saint-Lazare as a leper house.

Did God intend it, after all, as a shelter for the Company of the Mission?

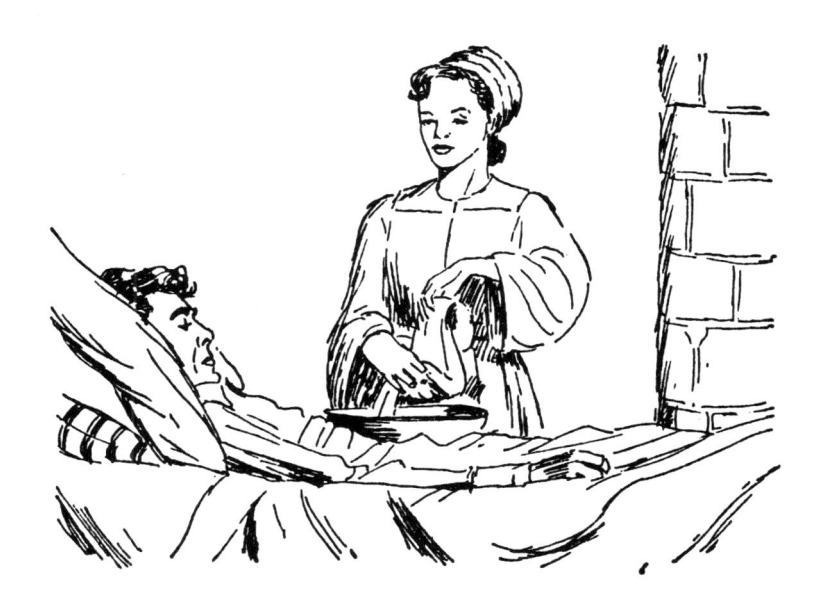

7

SAINT-LAZARE

ADRIAN LE BON kept his word. Within the next year he returned to the School of the Good Children more than thirty times and always received the same answer. Vincent would not move his Company to Saint-Lazare. Pierre de Bérulle had died in 1629, and now there was no one whose advice Vincent would have felt bound to follow. All the pleadings of le Bon's friends were of no avail.

Finally, on a visit toward the end of 1631, the prior

lost his temper. "Sir, all my monks stand with me in this matter. So do all your friends, as you well know. Do you feel then, Monsieur, that everybody else is wrong, and you are right?"

He could not have made a more barbed thrust. Vincent, almost in panic, hurried off to the chapel. Was his humility a form of pride? Once again, did he want to do everything for himself so that he might have all the credit?

Vincent prayed most of the night. The next day he sent word to the prior that he would accept Saint-Lazare, but on the Company's own terms. The mission priests must live entirely apart from the monks. No new members were to be taken in by the Augustinians, so that eventually Saint-Lazare would belong to the missionaries. Adrian le Bon would remain as prior, but he would have no authority whatever over Vincent's Company.

On January 8, 1632, Vincent and his priests moved their meager possessions into the great domain of Saint-Lazare. It was an almost frightening change from the cramped rooms of the School of the Good Children. Ceilings were lofty, windows were large, and sunlight fell in huge blocks into corridors as long as those in the king's palace. Several families lived inside the enclosure and made their living by the gardening and care of the livestock. Beggars crowded to the kitchen door for the time when food would be handed out. A house of detention in which young rakes of noble blood had been placed by their families had, under Adrian le Bon, become a prison. Vincent set about at once to make it a house of correction, and many young men left it in the future to enter the religious life. The prison itself became a model for humane treatment and justice. Vincent's "guests", as he called the one leper and the insane in the garden huts, received his personal attention. His mission priests had to be instructed and their next work planned.

In the midst of all this activity, Vincent managed to keep the daily rule for his Congregation. They arose always at four in the morning and a half hour later were in the chapel, where they remained for prayers and Mass until nine o'clock. At eleven they had their dinner, then an hour's recreation, then silence until after supper, when they had another hour of recreation, then prayers and silence again until after Mass the next day. All available time was spent in study and preparation for the work ahead.

Louise de Marillac and Margaret were joined by other girls from the country. The house near the School of the Good Children became too small, and a larger house was found in the Street of La Chapelle, near the lovely chapel built by Saint Louis. Working from five in the morning until ten at night, they accomplished marvels. Destitute families were flocking into Paris from the war-ridden provinces. The Ladies of Charity, working side by side with Louise's girls, gave up their social life to devote all their time to charity, and still there was too much to do.

It was surprising, in view of this, that the dainty Madame Goussaulte should suggest to Vincent that they take on another burden.

"Do you realize the state of things at the Charity Hospital, sir?" she demanded. "A sick person must make his confession before he can be admitted, and the sacrament has become a tool to gain entry!"

"I know it well, Madame", Vincent replied. "But the hospital is under the charge of the Order of Saint Victor. I could not interfere."

Madame wasted no more arguments but went straight to the archbishop of Paris. He was easily won over. A day or two later, Vincent received a letter from the archbishop. He was to do all he could to reform conditions in the hospital. Taking the order to "reform" as widely as he could, Vincent enlisted the Ladies of Charity, along with Louise's girls, to improve the nursing care also. The ladies were delighted. Work at the hospital became their new game. But the game ended abruptly with the sudden onslaught of the plague.

Overnight, beggars and thieves never seen in the daytime lay dying in the streets. People rushed back to their homes only to find that some member of their own family had been stricken in their absence. Inside of a day the hospital beds were filled, and patients lay on the straw-covered floors. The dead were too numerous for other than mass burial. At Saint-Lazare, the line of people waiting for soup suddenly vanished, for those who had not taken ill had escaped to the country. Vincent and his priests were at the hospital day and night. It was the custom of the time to guard against infection by wearing a mask, a coat, and gloves soaked in oil and herbs and to hold garlic in the mouth. The priests did none of this. Not one contracted the terrible disease.

Louise and her girls, also in their usual garb of blue-gray with white apron and turban, were not so fortunate. Little Margaret Naseau was the first to die. Finding no room in the hospital, she had taken a sick woman into her own bed. The woman had recovered, but Margaret, already ill herself, had died within a few days. Soon to follow her were Nicolette, Claudine, and little Andrea, who was afraid she had sinned because she loved her work so much. But Louise weathered the terrible times with nothing worse than headaches and exhaustion. Side by side with her girls she nursed the sick, prayed with the dying, and closed the eyes of the dead. When the plague had run its course and disappeared as mysteriously as it had come, she came to Vincent with a request.

It was a cold November day of 1633. Louise was pale and thinner than ever, but through the awful days she had found heroic peace in leaving all to God. Now, she told Vincent, she felt that the time had come to take another step for her little company of girls.

"I have too many friends among the ladies of the court", she said, smiling a little wryly. "They keep demanding that I let a few of my girls go to them, but they did not forsake their fathers' houses to become maids for rich ladies. The only remedy I see, Monsieur, is for all of us—the girls in Paris and the ones in the country confraternities who have joined our group—to be permitted to take some kind of vows to bind us together. Then there would be no danger of the girls being talked into leaving, for the superior would make the decisions. And we need the spiritual bond it would give us." Louise's pale face glowed. "The very power of physical fatigue must be overcome! We work such long days and get so tired, and with other days coming up exactly like them—oh, we need a definite rule, Monsieur!"

"You don't want your girls to become nuns", Vincent said. "Nuns are cloistered. Francis de Sales wanted his Visitation nuns to be able to leave their convent and work among the poor, but the Holy Father would not permit it, and so they ended up in the cloister. That must not happen to you."

"Heavens, no, Monsieur!"

"But I agree that some sort of bond is needed now. Call the girls in from all the confraternities, Mademoiselle, for a—well, let us call it a seminary. Work out an order of the day for them, times for rising, meals, prayers, so that when they return to their posts they will have a rule to live by."

"But no vows, Monsieur?"

"Not yet. For the moment, let their only vows be to serve the poor and the sick and to teach the children."

"What about their dress, Monsieur?"

"No veils", Vincent said instantly. "Veils and vows

would make religious out of them, and religious must be cloistered."

"And the veils would only get in the way of their scrubbing", Louise said practically. "There will be no special convent, either, except for my house, which will be the motherhouse here in Paris. The girls in the confraternities will go on living in the homes of parishioners, just as they have been doing. The procurator general should be delighted with such an economical company!"

But the procurator general, when approached by Vincent, was shocked. The idea, like Vincent's first undertaking of the mission priests, was too revolutionary. Mademoiselle le Gras might draw up whatever rules she felt might be for the good of her company, and the girls should continue with the confraternities as parish workers. But formal recognition could not be given them, for—what in the world were they? Not nuns, not quite seculars. What, then?

"They are servants of the poor, Monsieur", Vincent said. And he went away leaving the procurator general somewhat baffled.

On November 29, in the chapel of Saint-Lazare, Vincent gave the first of his conferences for the Little Sisters, as he had begun to call them. Every week or two until his death he would continue this practice. Louise sat among them just as she had worked among them from the first, their mother and their example.

"The good that God wishes to be done will be done

without our thinking about it", he told them. "For God will use us, and we are not to be concerned as to how or where or when. But we do know that to do his work, you must not be shut away. Your cloister will be the house of the sick, your cell a room in someone's poor hut, your chapel the parish church. You will make your meditations while you are hurrying along the streets of the city instead of strolling in some quiet cloister walk. You will be surrounded by the temptations of the world, my daughters, and so you must remember all the more that you are servants of God."

Vincent paused, for a pretty little face was showing signs of weeping.

"What is it, my dear?" he asked gently. "Something you would like to tell me?"

"I stopped to watch a street fair only yesterday, Monsieur! The music was so lively, and before I knew it, I was tapping my feet! Oh, I was wicked, *wicked*! How will I ever do enough penance for it?"

Vincent had to hold his lips very firmly to keep back a smile. This was little Margaret of Saint Lawrence, who was only seventeen and most likely never had seen a street fair.

"Well, now that you have watched a fair, you will not be tempted to stop again, will you, my daughter? Of course not. But see how careful we must be? A nun in a cloister would never have the distraction of a street fair!"

Even little Margaret laughed.

"The nun's aim in life is her own salvation", Vincent

went on. "But yours is the salvation of your neighbor. You must have strength to carry out your vocation."

With her girls, Louise worked out a routine for the day. There were stated times for Mass and prayers, but service to the poor came first.

"If a hungry man knocks at the door when we are at prayers," she told the girls, "then one must leave to feed him. The poor are all we have to get us to heaven, and we can never do enough for them. Some of you will return now to your former places, some will go to new places—but God will be with all of us. His blessing on you!"

The parish priests received these religious who were not nuns with delight. Now they had someone to teach catechism, to make parish visits, to bring worthy causes of charity to their attention—to do all the drudgery there had been no one to do before. Never had mean tasks been done so joyously. Soon priests from far parishes were sending girls of melancholy temperament to Louise to make over. Nearly all of these were sent home. From the upper classes, and even from the nobility, a number of young women begged admittance to the house in La Chapelle. Vincent and Louise both laid all the difficulties before them: the work was geared to peasant strength, and no one would be excused from it. Poverty was not romantic when endured day after day. Yet the cultured girls, far from being discouraged, joined the company, and several became Louise's trusted administrators.

In the meantime, Vincent was deeply occupied with his affairs at Saint-Lazare. The archbishop of Paris, in transferring the estate to the Congregation, had stipulated that young men about to be ordained to the priesthood must first be given a retreat of two weeks at Saint-Lazare. There was no mention of pay for these guests, who might number five hundred a year. Vincent was undaunted. When the larder became empty, the Lord would provide. The state of the priesthood was shameful, and the only reformation that could be brought about would be through the young men. The middle-aged, indolent parish priests were not going to mend their ways, and there was no hope for the bishops who were never consecrated and who later married. On the young priests rested the salvation of the Church. There were no proper seminaries even yet, and although two weeks with Vincent would be better than nothing, the problem still remained.

Immediately, however, as with everything Vincent did, the fame of the retreats flared over Paris. A rich woman offered to pay the entire cost for the first five years, a magnificent gift since the numbers were bound to grow. The queen, Anne of Austria, attended one of the sessions and was so inspired that she offered to pay for the next five years.

"So we have hardly begun, and yet we have our expenses taken care of for the next ten years", Vincent said to Anthony Portail. "My only motive in the retreats is to provide young priests who will go into the parishes and continue where our missionaries leave off, for a mission is only a spurt, and the daily work must be carried on. But God seems to be nudging us again. What will he think of next, Anthony?"

"Perhaps a seminary, sir?" Anthony said timidly.

Vincent's eyes twinkled. Francis de Sales had worked for seventeen years to produce three priests and had finished, he said, with one and a half.

Nevertheless, in 1636, Vincent made his attempt. In the old School of the Good Children, he opened a seminary. The movement was started. Out in the renegade parish of Saint-Sulpice, the ambitious young pastor founded another. Then two more were opened under different heads. Since the bishops would do nothing and were themselves the most ignorant and loose living, reform of the clergy had seemed impossible until Vincent undertook it. Now some of the priests who were not immoral but had merely fallen in with the prevailing laxity were invited by Vincent to what came to be known as the Tuesday Conferences. A man had to be of good character and sincere in his desire to serve God well. Carefully picked by Vincent, these men made an eight-day retreat at Saint-Lazare. Thereafter, attendance each Tuesday was so compulsory that anyone who did not attend must send in an essay on the subject to be discussed. All were encouraged to speak, but without oratory, on the Christian virtues most necessary to the priesthood. At the end of the session Vincent, almost timid in his humility, would make a summary of the points they had discussed.

Men felt honored to belong to the Tuesday Conferences, for the numbers were very small. In twenty years, only 250 would be accepted. The effect on the lives and preaching of the members was immediately seen. Cardinal Richelieu, who had given a thousand crowns toward the establishment of Vincent's seminary, attended several of the conferences and was so impressed that he asked Vincent for a list of the men who would make good bishops. Far from pleased, the peasant priest agreed only after the cardinal swore that the information would be kept secret. The Tuesday Conferences were not going to become a stepping-stone to bishoprics. So thorough was Vincent's teaching of humility that several priests refused bishoprics, preferring to carry out the work that was so steadily growing, that of assisting the members of the Congregation on their missions.

Since the Congregation was dedicated to work in the country, the Conference priests turned to giving missions in the city. One of these, given at Saint-Germaine-in-the-Woods for the royal court, was attended by King Louis XIII. He was so impressed that he proclaimed the Blessed Virgin the patron of France. It was no uncommon thing for the priests to go from such gatherings straight to the Charity Hospital, where they would hear the confessions of dying beggars, or to visit the poor and the sick in their homes. No service was beneath them.

"Saint-Lazare must have a magic light!" the archbishop of Paris said to Vincent after one of the Tuesday meetings. "These men flock here like moths to a flame!"

"The power of virtue is the flame", Vincent said quietly. "When its light falters and grows dim, they will desert us."

The light glowed and increased in brightness. In the days to come, Saint-Lazare would be the only candle aflame in the darkness of France, and its rays would penetrate into every corner of the suffering kingdom.

8

THE FIRST FOUNDLING

ON A LATE SUMMER AFTERNOON in 1638, Vincent left the Convent of the Visitation, where he had just finished one of his periodic conferences with the superior, and trudged along the Street of Saint-Jacques toward the Island of the City. He should stop at the School of the Good Children to see how things were going for his seminarians, and the sick at the Charity Hospital would be looking for him, too. But this evening he must preach to his Company, gathered for retreat, and preparation of the sermon was most important. So much depended upon the Company now. . . .

Vincent would have liked to hurry toward home, but it seemed that everyone he met must stop him—women to tell him that without the food from Saint-Lazare their children would be dead, beggars to complain that they were too sick to work, men and women praising him before they would beg for more help. The praise embarrassed him, but he could not blame them when they asked for more to eat. Even the enormous amount of food dispensed daily from all his charities in Paris could not satisfy the starving people. Nothing but manna from heaven could supply the need. Everywhere there were want and hunger.

Except in the royal palace. Vincent, slipping out of the crowded Street of the Tanners, came close to the wall. A great gate stood open, giving a wide view of the courtyard. There was a crowd inside, but, unlike the ragged rabble in the street, these men were dressed in fine attire. In the middle of the indolent, laughing group, with his sleeves rolled up and a leather apron tied around him, was the king. He was shoeing a horse. Several blacksmiths were in attendance, but the horse's hoof rested on the king's knee and he was driving in the nails himself.

One of the courtiers called a greeting to Vincent, but he pretended not to hear. He harbored no bitterness toward the king, for royalty made a man above criticism. But France had sore need of a good and understanding ruler. It seemed ironic that her monarch should spend his time shoeing horses, cutting his courtiers' hair, and painting and cooking, while his country bled to death under Richelieu's hand.

For that was what was happening. Back in 1617 young Louis, wanting to be king in more than name, had seen to it that the man who stood in his way was assassinated. Then, having installed Cardinal Richelieu as his prime minister, he proceeded to forget all the obligations of the throne. The cardinal approved of this. Now he ruled France.

Richelieu first set about breaking the power of the nobles. For centuries they had been absolute rulers in their counties and duchies, swearing allegiance to the king only when it suited them. Those who would not submit to Richelieu found the army at their doors ready to lay siege. The others, who gave up their powers, found themselves with nothing to do at home, and they moved to Paris, where they lived in beautiful villas and became hangers-on at court. Never had the city seen so much wealth.

Never, too, had it seen so much poverty. Richelieu's demands for taxes were without mercy or common sense. Employers, having paid their taxes, had nothing left to pay their workers, and so the small industries of lace making and glass and cloth manufacturing were closing down. The workers, hungry, drifted into Paris. Others, numbering into the thousands, remained starving where they were.

It was for these, out of reach of the charities, that

Vincent felt the greatest anxiety. And with his customary genius he found a practical solution. His work as royal almoner brought him naturally into contact with the court and the nobility, and he persuaded not only the Ladies of Charity but the queen, indolent and frivolous Anne of Austria, to give him large sums to distribute to the poor. They responded so wholeheartedly that the confraternities were the salvation of France.

Vincent thought of all this as he tramped along the road to Saint-Denis, which would bring him home. He had heard today of a new recipe for soup that seemed even more economical and nourishing than the others he had recommended: coarse bread, lentils, dried peas, seasonings, butter, and salt. Out in the provinces, of course, some of these things might not be available, even if money was provided to buy them. Brother Matthew had been miraculously successful in carrying funds into the provinces. But there could come a time when he would be outwitted and might lose not only his purse but his life. He should have been home yesterday at the latest from his last trip into Picardy. Thinking of him, Vincent increased his limping pace to a one-sided trot.

It was a great relief to come into the courtyard of Saint-Lazare and see Brother Matthew, evidently just arrived, taking the saddle bags off his little donkey. He never rode the donkey, but used it to carry his supplies. The heat and the swarming flies told Vincent that this time the brother had carried home a load of fish.

"How did it go this time, Matthew?" Vincent asked as he hurried forward.

Brother Matthew's eyes lighted, and a smile broadened his round face. "We outwitted them again, Monsieur, my little donkey and I. One time, though, we were almost caught."

"Tell me about it, Brother", said Vincent.

Brother Matthew's adventures, recounted in the security of Saint-Lazare, were often comical, but neither man was deceived by a funny story. Every step of the way had held its own danger. The country was infested with soldiers, who robbed and plundered as the only means of keeping alive themselves. For five years now Brother Matthew had been carrying funds to the confraternities in the provinces, and his dumpy figure trudging along with the donkey had become a well-known sight. The brother, the robbers knew, often carried large sums of money, and they lay in wait for him. A religious habit was no defense for a man or woman in these terrible times. But Brother Matthew had an innocent look that was most disarming, and he glanced up at his superior now with that trusting air of a child.

"We walked right into the middle of a band of soldiers once, Monsieur, but I had seen them ahead on the road, and I dropped my purse into a thicket of brambles. So I could tell them I was a penniless friar. They believed me, after they searched me and found nothing. It delayed us, though, because we had to go back and find the purse after dark. Quite a scramble."

"You were on your way to Bohain then, Brother?"

"Yes, Monsieur. We are feeding eleven hundred people a day at Bohain alone, and at Saint-Quentin there are fifteen hundred sick. Remember how Picardy used to be, Monsieur, flocks of sheep everywhere? Now you don't even see the bones." Brother Matthew stroked the little donkey, and the touch was so familiar that the sleepy eyes did not twitch. "The looms of Picardy are empty; in Burgundy and Champagne the wine presses stand useless. Nowhere I go do I see anything but misery and death. Where will it all end, Monsieur?"

"When in God's eyes it is enough, then it will end", Vincent said. "Perhaps for France this is the dark night of the soul. Well, rest yourself and the donkey, Brother. Tomorrow you will have to start into Normandy."

Vincent crossed the courtyard and entered the large building that contained all the living apartments. Making his way quickly to his own bare little cell, he shut himself in. He must work at his sermon. But Brother Matthew's question burned in his brain. Where would it all end? France was now enduring not only civil war but a threat from the outside as well. Ferdinand of Austria had been for twenty years an ally of the Catholic rulers of Germany and Spain, and together they had been fighting all the Protestant powers with the aim of bringing them into the same alliance. For the past four years Ferdinand had been making forays into France. Richelieu, alarmed at last, left off his war with the nobles and sought their support against the foreign enemy. Some of the noblemen refused to join him. So confused was the situation now that the entire country was in a turmoil, and those who suffered most were the poor, who had no understanding of what the war was all about.

It was difficult for Vincent to keep his mind on his sermon that night. As soon as the services were over, he let himself out of the side gate and tramped once again along the road to Saint-Denis. The sick in the hospital would be disappointed that he had not come to them today. They were his children, and he could not rest until he had seen them.

Paris was never safe at night; but especially since the influx from the country none of the city dwellers ventured out after dark. Many of the people were peasants who came to Paris because here they would be saved from starvation, but many more were beggars and cutthroats who surged in to make their evil harvest. Their dens were the old stone quarries and saltpeter works out at the edge of the city, where even the king's archers dared not disturb them. As soon as darkness fell, they would begin to skulk in through the narrow old streets. There was no lighting of any kind, except a candle gleaming in a window once in a while. The night watchman, mounted on a horse, would ride regularly on his rounds, a flaring torch held high. The light and the clatter of hoofs on the cobblestones were actually the watchman's weapon, for with these warnings of his approach the ruffians would hide. Neither they nor the watchman wanted an encounter.

The First Foundling

Vincent never gave a thought to his own safety. Paris was as well known to him by night as by day. With his little lantern, wearing no cape because the night was warm, he was a shadow slipping through other shadows. Music drifted out to him over the palace wall when he reached the Island. The queen was having another of her parties. It might be well to call on her tomorrow. After a lavish entertainment she would often ease her conscience by giving Vincent a like sum for his charities. . . .

"Stop, or your life!" a rough shout came out of the night. Vincent stopped. He raised the lantern, not to let him see who had spoken but to light his own face. There was a mumbling in the blackness. After a moment Vincent lowered the light and plodded on. Such an occurrence was so common that he hardly wasted a thought on it.

He had gone only a few yards farther when he was stopped again. Patiently lifting the lantern, he waited. This time a wolfish creature came forward into the light. His hair was long and matted with the straw he had slept in during the day, his clothing was rags, but the most arresting thing about him was that in the crook of his arm he held a small baby wrapped in a dirty cloth. The little face was pinched, the eyes closed.

"Is the child dead?" Vincent asked quickly.

"Not yet. Baptize him, Monsieur?"

"Of course. Come with me to the hospital."

The wretch thrust the small bundle at Vincent. How

light it felt, and how frail. If the baby breathed, the rise and fall of its chest was too tiny to be seen.

"We'll have to be quick", Vincent said.

But the man was gone. The baby was clinging to Vincent's old cassock with a hand no bigger than a thumb.

Holding the lantern out before him, Vincent made the best time he could to the hospital chapel. Every night babies were left abandoned in dark corners of the old streets, and the hospital was full of the sick ones.

"This one is not sick, just hungry", the Little Sister said when she looked at the baby. "We have so many now. Why don't you bring him to the home for the foundlings in the street of Saint-Landry, Monsieur?"

Vincent went reluctantly, for weird stories concerning the refuge for foundlings circulated around Paris. The moment the door was opened, he knew the stories had truth to them. A heavy, sweet odor was wafted out, the odor of deadening drugs used in the hospital.

"Another one?" the woman grumbled. "Haven't I got enough already?"

"I have no way to care for a baby at the mission", Vincent said.

"The mission? So you're Monsieur Vincent! I've heard about you." She took the baby, and the tiny hand parted from the fold of the cassock with a little scratching sound. "Strong little beggar. Where did you pick him up?"

Vincent explained. "I baptized him", he added.

"Oh? We don't bother about baptism here. I can't be running to the priest every day. I have forty babies here sometimes, and two no-good girls to help me." The woman tossed her untidy head as if she would ward off his criticism. "Why don't you speak to the queen about it, Monsieur? I've heard you have her ear whenever you need it!"

Vincent bowed his head humbly, his usual reply to rudeness. The baby gave a weak cry.

"You should feed him, M'amselle, so he won't wake the others."

"He'll be quiet after he's had a drop of laudanum." She scowled crossly. "I've got to keep them quiet so I can get my rest! Do you think I'm going to coddle them all day and all night, too?"

She shut the door with a bang. Vincent lingered uncertainly, on the point of knocking and asking to take the baby back again. But he had no place for the poor little creature. The refuge was better than nothing.

True to his custom of taking his time, Vincent thought long and carefully about the place on the street of Saint-Landry. As the king's almoner, he could have had it abolished instantly, but that was not his way. Never rush into anything; make certain first that God is opening a door and not merely making a peephole in a stone wall.

Going out often after dark, as he had to do, Vincent kept a careful watch for abandoned children. Every night he came upon at least one. The watchman, perhaps feeling sorry for the tiny helpless things, would sometimes pick up a baby and carry it with him on his horse until he came upon Vincent. Once in a while a ragged woman would hand over a child directly, but there might be questions then as to whether the little one was hers, and it was much simpler to watch for the bobbing lantern and leave the bundle in Vincent's path. There was nothing for Vincent to do but baptize the baby and carry it to the woman in Saint-Landry. Each time he did it, he felt that he was abandoning the child to the devil.

When at last Vincent decided what must be done, he moved quickly. Calling a meeting of his Ladies of Charity, he had hardly laid the problem before them when the first purse was opened and the fund begun amid tenderhearted tears. The emotional ladies, some of whom were childless, took up the cause with such enthusiasm that within a few days they had secured a house in the neighborhood of the School of the Good Children, near the Gate of Saint-Victor. Louise's girls set about scrubbing it from top to bottom. The ladies brought furniture and the outgrown clothes of their own babies. Children would not be taken away from Saint-Landry, Vincent ruled, but no more would be brought there. All of the abandoned babies would hereafter be under the care of the Little Sisters. The girls were too well disciplined to beg assignment to the new project, but those selected were delighted beyond measure. In a short time there were twelve babies in the new home, and the ladies would drop in to help with them, and Vincent would stop whenever he passed. Louise herself spent all the time she could spare.

With the affectionate care the little ones grew strong and healthy, and that in itself presented a problem, for soon the house became too small. Some children were adopted into new homes, but not in the same numbers that they were admitted. The financial burden was finally so heavy that even the kindest hearted of the ladies began to wonder if they might not relinquish it.

"You have saved these children from almost certain death", Vincent told them. "Would you now desert them and leave them homeless?"

The answer, of course, was "No, Monsieur!" The great work was continued.

9

FRIEND OF THE KING

THE FEBRUARY DAY was cold. Snow had fallen the night before, and the city was bleak with winter. Vincent, huddled in the king's velvet-lined carriage, was driven swiftly along. He would have preferred to walk the miles to the palace at Saint-Germaine-in-the-Woods, but the queen had sent the carriage with a message to make haste. The king's illness had become much worse overnight, and she was afraid that he was dying.

Vincent peered out between the heavy curtains. They were crossing the last bridge over the Seine. A group of

Friend of the King

peasants, blue with cold, hugged the rail as the horses lurched past. The winter was terrible for the starving people. At Saint-Lazare the lines were so long there was never a time when the soup kettles were not bubbling. Richelieu had died in December of 1642, but the two months since the end of his reign had seen no change because the cardinal was hardly laid in his tomb before the king's infirmity began. If the prime minister's passing was to bring about any betterment, it would not be until the court knew what was to happen to the king.

The carriage rattled into the courtyard, its thunder suddenly deadened by the straw that had been scattered. The sick man must have quiet. Jerking the tail of his worn cape after him, Vincent clambered out of the carriage. The old wounds from his slave chains were bothering him again, and he limped. He was sixty-two now, his hair white, his body thinner than ever because in these years of want he ate even less than the peasants who were fed from the kitchen at Saint-Lazare. He did not like coming to the palace. But he had not come to serve a king, he reminded himself as he hurried after the liveried servant. He was here to bring comfort if he could to a dying man.

"The queen will see you first, Monsieur", the servant murmured and drew aside the heavy velvet curtain of a doorway. Vincent entered.

The setting was dramatically religious, for Anne of Austria, so called because she belonged to the Austrian House of Hapsburg, never did anything by halves. Now she was in a frenzy of prayer. Kneeling on a prie-dieu before a large crucifix, wearing the purple of sorrow, she grasped a rosary made of the largest pearls Vincent ever had seen. On either side of her in their solemn black knelt two nuns.

Vincent had talked often with the queen on matters of charity. Sometimes she would be impatient over being bothered, but always she was lazily agreeable to his suggestions for alms. He was her conscience, she had told him more than once, and his charities would get her into heaven.

Today she touched his heart as she never had before. She was not a pampered queen but a woman weeping for her husband.

"You must be with him when he goes, Monsieur", she said as she stood before him. "There are other priests here, of course, even the archbishop of Paris. But you are the one he must have. Promise me you will stay, Monsieur Vincent."

"I promise, Madame", Vincent said, although reluctantly.

His stay was spun out into a week, and at the end of that time Louis was better. Deep inside he was a religious man, and he had repented sadly for his neglect of his royal duties. If he were to live, Vincent thought, perhaps things would be different. With Louis' new recognition of what he must be to France and with his wife's attention to prayer, there would at last be a royal couple worthy of the name upon the throne.

But the improvement was short. Once again the king's carriage came racing to Saint-Lazare, and this time when Vincent walked into the royal chamber he knew that death was already sitting at the bedside. Louis XIII was only forty-two years old, yet he looked like an old man.

"Stay, Monsieur. With you beside me, I'll die well", he whispered.

Vincent pressed the thin hand. Anne and her nuns, courtiers, and priests knelt in the big room, but Vincent was alone with the king on the raised dais. Louis made his last confession and received Extreme Unction.

"I'm not afraid to die", he said then. "My only fear now is that at the end I may remember some kind of bitterness toward my wife. I forgive her for all her scheming against my people and me. I know she has always lied to me, but so much of it was my fault. I neglected her." Turning his head toward the window, he said with a little more strength, "Open it. I want to see Saint-Denis, where I am to lie forever."

A few days later, with all the pomp that had begun with the Emperor Charlemagne, Louis was entombed in the ancient abbey of Saint-Denis. He had died in Vincent's arms.

Two weeks after the funeral, Anne sent for Vincent again. She was back in the Palace of the City and somewhat heady with the power of being queen regent of France. For years, all her little connivings had been spied upon and reported to the king by Richelieu. Now she was not only free of criticism but assured of a long reign, since the dauphin was but four years old. Even in manner she was changed from the woman who had mourned her husband. She wore the white that was mourning for a queen, but it was resplendent white of heavy silk. All the furnishings of the chamber were white, and long white tapers glowed in a solid line beneath a portrait of the dead king.

Anne was the same age as Louis had been, and all the white was not becoming to her. Too many nights danced away had left lines of fatigue upon her face. Already, so the gossip ran, she was seeking entertainment, hiding among her ladies in waiting so she could watch the mummers and magicians. There was talk, too, that Mazarin, the Sicilian whom Richelieu had brought to court, was cleverly seeing to it that the queen was well supplied with entertainers.

"I am grateful to you, Monsieur, for your faithfulness to my husband", she said. "I ask now that you retain the same faithfulness toward me. I need your help." She paused, and Vincent merely waited. "I wish you to be my spiritual adviser, Monsieur."

The humble priest was stunned. The queen's confessor would have to be at her beck and call, a sort of spiritual lackey. Surely God would not require this of him!

"I need your services in another field also, sir", Anne continued, as if the first matter were already settled. "I am forming a group to be known as the Council of Conscience to advise me in all the business of the kingdom. You, sir, are to be in charge of ecclesiastical affairs."

"I am honored, Madame, but I cannot accept", Vincent said firmly. "I made a vow to serve the poor. My work is at Saint-Lazare."

"You're interested in the education of the clergy, are you not? You opened a seminary; you conduct retreats and your Tuesday Conferences. If you wish to see reform in the Church, how can you refuse?"

"I am only a humble priest, the son of a peasant, Madame."

"Then I wish we had more like you!"

"I haven't the time. You know the crowds that come daily to Saint-Lazare!"

"Do you make the soup with your own hands, sir?"

"It goes beyond soup, Madame."

The queen rose with a great rustling of silks, and Vincent backed out of her way.

"I am putting you on the Council, Monsieur, and that is the end of the matter. Louis would want it." She paused beside him, and her eyes filled with tears. "I cannot rule France without you, Monsieur!"

Vincent was beaten. Plodding through the lofty hall, he realized that to the very heart of him he was frightened. He wanted no part of court life. To be Anne's confessor, to have to rebuke her for the silly conduct which would most surely continue, this would be most embarrassing. And for a peasant, even a consecrated peasant, to mention to her that she should be careful not to incite gossip about herself and Mazarin, that was unthinkable.

He looked up suddenly to meet the regard of a slender, elegant gentleman who stood posed against the rich draperies of a doorway. Through the doorway came the music of a harp. The gentleman wore the brightest red velvet and taffeta, the breeches very short to show off his shapely legs, the surcoat slit over extravagant laces and embroidery. His pointed beard was carefully trimmed, his hair curled. The gaze he fastened on Vincent was amused, but in the thin-lipped smile there was a great deal of cruelty.

"So you have just left the queen, sir", he said, and his voice was light and soft, the kind that could flatter a woman or turn in a second to scorching sarcasm.

Although they never had met, Vincent knew him instantly—Jules Mazarin, to whom Richelieu had taught all his tricks. If the stories were true, he was already working himself into the confidence of the queen regent. As her spiritual adviser, Vincent must warn her about him. France could not endure another Richelieu.

"Welcome, Monsieur", Mazarin added, and the smile strengthened.

"Welcome to what, sir?"

"To the Council of Conscience."

Vincent knew he must have shown his consternation, for Mazarin raised an eyebrow.

"Didn't Her Majesty tell you? Oh, indeed, I was the first member she appointed to the Council. The head of it, in fact. If I may trust you with a secret, sir—" The smile became almost a laugh. "I am the new prime minister of France."

The harp music brightened. Vincent stared at the floor. How could the queen be sincere in her desire to reform the clergy when the man she had appointed prime minister was a powerful example of the very abuse that had brought the Church so low? Mazarin, cardinal of the Church and bishop of Metz, had never advanced beyond Minor Orders.

When Vincent finally raised his head, Mazarin was gone. His eyes fell on a small statue of the Agony in the Garden against the shadowy wall. He made the sign of the cross.

Resigned but deeply troubled, Vincent took his place on the Council. Mazarin was his bitter enemy from the first, for the cardinal had to continue his crafty use of bishoprics and clerical honors if he was to increase his own power. Wealthy bishoprics were often looked upon by the nobles as convenient berths for their younger sons, who would inherit nothing, because a man need not even be a priest in order to be a bishop. A vicar general would be appointed to administer the office, and the bishop need never go near the diocese himself. Babies were often appointed abbots, and again someone else would serve for them, and their only connection with the abbey would be to receive the revenue. Some of the women in religion were as indifferent as the men. Nuns might be found living outside the convents, adding ribbons and lace to their habits and joining in social doings. But these nuns were the daughters of nobles who had founded convents especially for them, and Mazarin would not tolerate any criticism that might disturb them.

"How many religious do we have in France, one hundred fifty thousand?" Vincent said one day to his secretary. "And there are one hundred thousand clergy. What number of these would you say, Brother Ducourneau, live good lives?"

"All but a thousand, two thousand, perhaps, among the religious. But the clergy..." The brother shrugged, spreading his hands.

"Exactly", said Vincent. "And we hear so little of the ones who live well. The world is much more interested in evil than in good." He sighed deeply. "Often, Brother, I feel that I am lighting a candle in the sun. The little flame is wasted."

"Indeed, not always, sir!" the brother protested.

When the nobility could not get what they wanted from Vincent in the way of ecclesiastical favors, they would sometimes take the roundabout course of obtaining the queen's sanction, in the hope that this would impress him. He had not been long in office when a certain lady in waiting, desiring the bishopric of Poitiers for her son, tried this method of approach. Bustling up to the door of Saint-Lazare, she demanded to see Vincent immediately. He was at his meal, but he left it to receive her.

"You are to sign this paper, sir", the duchess said quickly. "No, I cannot come in. I am in a great hurry today. It is the queen's wish that you sign it."

Vincent opened the paper. It was an order making the duchess' son the bishop of Poitiers. He knew the young man, who was not a priest, was a headstrong, spoiled ne'er-do-well often lying drunk in the streets. The king's archers had arrested him several times for his pranks.

"Madame, may I make a suggestion?" Vincent asked humbly.

"If you can make it quickly, sir. I haven't much time."

"Send your son to me, Madame. Let him be a guest for as long as we feel it necessary. Believe me, he will benefit far more than if he were given a bishopric."

The duchess began to swell. "If you mean by being a guest he would be detained in your house of correction, sir, you—why, you are insulting! You don't know my son! I'll be back tomorrow for the paper. Signed!"

And she turned and flounced back to her carriage.

That afternoon Vincent called on the queen regent. He seldom bothered Anne with the details of his appointments, but since this appointment was her own he felt obliged to bring it before her. The queen, as he had suspected, had actually paid no attention to the duchess' request.

"We were listening to music, Monsieur, and I scarcely heard what she said. But I did agree?"

"Yes, Madame", Vincent said quietly. There was so much more that he might have said about delivering the affairs of the Church into unworthy and blasphemous hands. But Mazarin, not the peasant priest, had the loudest voice these days.

"The duchess has a terrible temper", Anne said uneasily. "Would it not be better to—perhaps—"

"If your Council of Conscience is to function as if it has a conscience, Madame, then we must fear nothing. It would be a great sin against many people to do this thing."

The queen made a wry face. "I'd never dare tell the duchess that I've changed my mind!"

"Then I myself shall tell her, Madame."

Leaving the queen's presence, Vincent went straight to the duchess. She received him coyly, with much dainty laughter and fluttering of her fan. He passed her the paper, which she unfolded, then slapped down on the table before her.

"This paper is not signed by either you or the queen, Monsieur!"

"Indeed it is not, Madame."

"May I ask what you mean by this?"

Vincent straightened and took a long breath. "Madame, so long as I am a member of the queen's council, every bishop appointed by me will be a qualified priest and not a dissipated young man whose family would like to see him well away from Paris!"

It was a most outspoken statement for Vincent. Injustice to himself never bothered him, but injustice to the Church was a different matter.

Friend of the King

The duchess' face began to swell again with rage, a most unlovely sight. She was short and stocky, strong as a farm wife. Glancing about for a missile of some sort, her eye fell on a small footstool. She picked it up and flung it as hard as she could at Vincent.

He did not even duck, and the stool hit him squarely on the forehead. He returned to Saint-Lazare that day with blood streaming down his face.

That story also went the rounds of Paris, and the nobles who might have tried the same thing gave up the idea once and for all. Already the clergy had found that the most certain way not to be given a promotion was to hint to Monsieur Vincent about it. People had expected to see Saint-Lazare prosper, for it would be only natural for Vincent to appropriate a few benefices for the good of his community, but he did nothing of the kind.

"Poverty will not harm us, but riches would", he often said and continued on his day-to-day existence. When the treasury was empty, he rejoiced. Now, he said, they must depend completely on the Lord to keep them alive. They were never disappointed.

The priest in his peasant shoes and shabby cassock continued to sit with the richly attired Council, unhappy about the honor but bound to serve well. All over Paris the poor rejoiced because their beloved Monsieur Vincent had not permitted his contact with royalty to change him.

10

A RIDE IN THE NIGHT

VINCENT SAT AT HIS TABLE in his cold, bare little room, writing. Every day he spent long hours at his correspondence, for by this January of 1649 his work had gone beyond the borders of France, and he kept in touch through letters with every mission and confraternity. This alone was a huge undertaking. In addition, there was his anxiety about the War of the Fronde, now dragging into its sixth year.

"There is a rush of country folk into the city, and

those in the city rush to the country", he wrote. "Their misery and fear are so extreme that they think anywhere would be better than where they are. Each morning the drums begin beating at seven, calling for volunteers, but there are none because every able man has already joined the army. The Austrians are . . ."

Rubbing his head wearily, he laid down the pen. The great threat to France was not the Austrians but her own queen and the prime minister. Cleverly taking his time, by flattering Anne and assuring her that he was merely carrying out her own splendid plans, Mazarin had secured the reins of government to himself. The queen was lazy and only too happy to shrug off her duties. When any pressure of business was put upon her, she took to her bed until the business was attended to by someone else. She had a positive passion for the light entertainments of the day, and Mazarin highly approved. From his native Italy, a year or so ago, he had imported a company of entertainers so expensive that special taxes had to be levied to pay for them, and the people finally rebelled. They had despised Richelieu, but he had ruled with his own ideas of fairness. Mazarin had no tinge of fairness about him. He must be run out of France and the ruling power restored to the queen regent.

So the army, which should have been fighting the Austrians, left the battlefields and flocked to Paris under the leadership of Condé, the general who, many felt, should have been prime minister instead of Mazarin. It was a curious, mixed-up war. The answer, Vincent thought as his pen hovered over the paper, would be for Mazarin to resign and leave France. The people, who still revered the queen in spite of her stupidity, would then unite against their common enemy, Ferdinand of Austria.

But there was no point in setting down such conclusions in the letter to the superior of the confraternity at Bohain. "Let us leave all to God, my daughter", he finished. "In the meantime, see that you put everything that is nourishing into the soup, but remember too that there are many mouths, and it is better to feed all a little than a few well."

Signing the letter, he sealed it with wax, addressed it, and laid it on the large pile which Brother Matthew would carry away on his next journey. He opened his door and listened a moment; then, hearing no one in the hallway, he slipped out and down the stairs. Saint-Lazare in these days was a teeming mass of humanity, and Vincent could be delayed for his whole afternoon.

Out in the street, he hurried along with the quick, limping gait that had carried him all over France. He still went everywhere on foot. Today he must get out to the old Castle of Bicetre, where Louise was barricaded in with the older orphans and in fear of their lives. The castle had been the haunt of renegades and tramps until the queen, entreated by Vincent for a place to house the children older than babies, had given it over to Louise. The tramps were violent over being turned out of their lair. A fair distance from Paris, isolated in a wood, the castle was well beyond protection by the law. Louise had said it was no place for women and children alone. But the Ladies of Charity, who had done a heroic work in supporting the orphans all these years, had insisted it was safe. Vincent had listened to the ladies. But Louise, as usual, was right. She should never have accepted the queen's gift. The babies, petted and loved by the Little Sisters, were well taken care of in the Thirteen Houses built especially for them in the city. The other children must be rescued immediately from the haunted old castle.

Vincent was stopped so often even on the country road that his progress was slow. He shrank from meeting people now, for they all held him in positive veneration, and it embarrassed him to have women weeping his praises.

"What God wants done, he is doing through us", Vincent would tell them. "We are but the humble instruments and worth nothing in ourselves."

In the tumbledown old castle, banked in high-grown weeds and forest run riot, he found Louise and her Daughters and the children packed and ready to leave.

"We shall walk back to Paris, Monsieur", Louise declared. "We can take turns carrying the smaller children. Your presence is the only safeguard we need."

And so, with Vincent in the lead, the little procession set out for the city. A tramp or two glared at them from the tangled woods, and the young children clung to the women's skirts. But they had not gone far when the road began to swarm with people, all bound toward Paris. There was a mob spirit about them, and they were laughing and singing crude ballads about the queen and Mazarin.

"Hush your foul tongue!" Louise said to a loudly singing big lout. "Do you want children to hear such things?"

"Children? I want the queen to hear me!" the fellow roared. "Louder, my wights! Worry her until she throws the Sicilian out of Paris!"

Louise set her mouth in disgust. "I wouldn't give a sou for the queen's safety tonight!" she said to Vincent. "The next hours will tell the tale."

Vincent tramped on in silence. He never uttered a word concerning the political situation. Only in that manner, taking no side, could he serve the people as he wished to do.

With Louise and the children housed safely in the crowded quarters they had left to go to Bicetre, Vincent returned to Saint-Lazare. But he did not lie down on his hard bed that night. The roar of the mob around the Royal Palace drifted clear out along the road to Saint-Denis, and the bonfires leaped so high that even at that distance the whole Island of the City appeared to be aflame.

In the morning, the news was flashed around that the queen, with the dauphin, had escaped somehow in disguise and was safe at the palace of Saint-Germaine-in-the-Woods. Now Paris was infuriated. The Parlement met and remained in continuous session, for they represented the people against the queen. General Condé, although he hated Mazarin, nevertheless now took command of the royal army and laid siege to Paris. The Parlement, the voice of the people, was going to be made to sing a different tune. All that Condé had to do was to maintain his forces in a tight ring around the city. With food supplies cut off, Paris would very soon fall from starvation.

Vincent and his Company, in the security of Saint-Lazare, could outlive any siege, for in the granaries and kitchens were supplies meant to feed hundreds. If he were to remain neutral in this civil war, he would face no criticism. His activities on the Council of Conscience and his friendship with the queen regent were well known, but it was also known that he used this friendship for the good of the poor and the betterment of the Church. By continuing to dispense food and to minister to their spiritual needs, he would be of immense service to the people of Paris. With a clear conscience, Vincent could have stood aside from the rebellion.

But he decided otherwise. In the late afternoon of January 14, a week after the siege had started, he called his secretary into his little cell and closed the door. Brother Ducourneau, thinking he had been summoned for a report of the day's work, began immediately.

"We fed over two thousand today, Father—"

Vincent held up his hand. "Prepare horses for us, Brother. Have them saddled and ready in the enclosure as soon as night prayers are over. Tonight we ride to Saint-Germaine-in-the-Woods."

Ducourneau's mouth dropped open. A less disciplined man would have protested. He did not. In the black of night, in a cold sleeting rain that would soon turn to snow, the two set out for the palace in which Louis XIII had died.

The ride was perilous. Chuckholes in the road were filled with water and discovered only when the horses stumbled into them, and the road itself was invisible in the dark. Once they had left Paris behind, they were in the encampment of Condé's forces. A few small fires glowed off in the woods, but the travelers were not challenged.

"They are so sure no one can escape from Paris that they don't even guard the road!" Ducourneau said. "We'll have no trouble."

But at Clichy they were attacked by a band of the ruffians who followed the army to steal and pillage, and a knife was at Vincent's throat when Ducourneau shouted out who they were. They were instantly released and let pass. Three times they had to cross the meandering Seine, and the last crossing was made on a bridge that the flood had loosened so it gave way under them, and the horses had to flounder ashore as best they could. The two riders were soaked to the skin. Arriving at the palace, Vincent asked to be taken to the queen even though it was the middle of the night. Perhaps thinking that he had come as a messenger to surrender Paris, she received him at once.

A Ride in the Night

The servant had offered him dry clothing, but he had not taken the time to attend to his own needs. He entered the presence of the queen dripping and muddy. She had not been aroused from sleep, for she was dressed in magnificent cloth of gold and jewels. No doubt she had just stepped out of the ballroom. Mazarin would see to it that she would not be bothered about the war.

Vincent came straight to the point. He described the misery and desperation of the people, the plundering that was going on in Paris. Anne listened attentively but with too much politeness. She was not going to permit herself to be impressed.

"Madame, you can be the savior of Paris!" Vincent said passionately. "If you act now you will save not only Paris but all of France. People will bless the name of Anne of Austria as they bless Joan of Arc!"

"Exactly what is it you wish me to do, Monsieur?" the queen asked.

Vincent drew a long breath. This would be what he had come to say. "Dismiss your prime minister, Madame. Send him out of the country."

He had thought she might be offended at his audacity, most certainly angry. But she appeared not even to be surprised. She tapped the jeweled fan lightly on the arm of her chair, not meeting his eyes.

"Perhaps that would end the siege, Monsieur", she said as casually as if she were discussing the weather. "And I would like to be back in Paris. The war is very annoying."

Vincent closed his lips tightly on a rebuke. Apparently Anne had forgotten that barely a week ago she had fled from the city to save her life and the dauphin's.

"I never make such decisions myself, Monsieur, as you well know. I suggest you speak with the cardinal himself. He is here at Saint-Germaine."

"Surely you could not think, Madame, that Mazarin would banish himself?"

The queen shrugged impatiently. "If it is for the good of France!"

Vincent bowed and backed out of the room. Anne, although she was stubbornly bedazzled by the clever Italian, could hardly believe that he had ever had the good of France at heart. She was up to her usual trick of refusing to make a decision.

It was futile, Vincent knew, to waste time on Mazarin, but he was determined to see his mission through. He asked for an audience and was received immediately. The cardinal was also in the most magnificent court dress. In the small room he looked at Vincent across the single candle on the table, and his eyes glowed like a cat's eyes watching a mouse.

"You and the queen together could give our country a great example of humility, sir", Vincent ended his plea. "Her sacrifice of your services, your own sacrifice of your high office would not only end the war but be a model of Christlike mortification!"

The candle flame reflected in Mazarin's eyes like other fires burning within him.

"And what would become of me, sir?" he asked quietly.

"You could return to your native Sicily, Your Eminence."

Mazarin's brows went up, and he pursed his thin lips. But he spoke with his former mildness. "You put it bluntly, sir."

"There is no time to do otherwise."

The cardinal turned to leave the room. Vincent could not let him go like this, even though he knew how fruitless any more talk would be.

"Your Eminence?"

Mazarin paused, again facing Vincent.

"You will consider my suggestion, sir?" Vincent asked humbly.

"Consider it? Oh, indeed! In fact, I'll speak with my advisers about it tomorrow. Good night, sir." The cardinal spoke softly, and he seemed to be holding back laughter.

Mazarin had no advisers. The whole royal court would be laughing with him tomorrow.

Vincent, too heartsick for rest, would have returned to Paris that night through the rain, but Brother Ducourneau persuaded him to accept shelter at Saint-Germaine. It was well that he did. In the morning, so early that Vincent had just finished saying Mass, Anthony Portail came plunging on horseback across the swollen river and into the courtyard of the palace. He had terrible news. Saint-Lazare, the single oasis of peace in the besieged city, had been looted by a furious mob, the granaries broken into and the supplies carried off. In their rage the throng had demanded Vincent himself and had stormed about until they were satisfied he was not there.

"But why?" Vincent asked the trembling Anthony. "What did they want of me?"

"Somehow, sir, they found out you had left Paris and come here, and they thought you had deserted to the queen's side!"

Vincent sat down on the chair Brother Ducourneau pushed hastily forward. They were in the little room where he was unvesting after Mass, and he still wore the white linen alb. His face was nearly as white as the linen.

"I was not worthy", he whispered. "I failed because I was not worthy of carrying out so important a trust. But I thought God wanted me to try!"

"Let me go back and tell everyone!" Anthony choked, his boyish face wet with tears and rain.

"What would you tell them, my son? That I will be banished from court instead of Mazarin because I dared speak against him? Or that I have shut myself out of Paris by trying to serve the people? No, Anthony. Tell them nothing."

"But you can't be blamed for failing! Mazarin would never give up!"

"If I had it to do over, I would have to make the attempt again. I couldn't rest without at least speaking to the queen about her terrible error in judgment."

A Ride in the Night

Vincent stood up and began taking off the alb, and Ducourneau jumped to help him.

"What will you do now, Monsieur?" the brother asked.

"Please don't come back to Saint-Lazare!" Anthony protested, as if he feared this turning of the other cheek was exactly what Vincent might do. "If you could stay here for a time—"

"No, Anthony. I'll go out into the provinces and visit our confraternities. If God shuts me out of Paris for a time, it is because he has need of me elsewhere."

So Brother Ducourneau and Anthony said good-bye to their superior at the gates of Saint-Germaine and watched him ride off alone toward Villepreux, the nearest of the confraternities. Vincent was disappointed, naturally, that his mission to the queen regent had been so unfruitful. But God had wanted him to make the attempt, of that he was certain. He had failed because somewhere in him there was an unworthiness that must be burned away. Perhaps, in some slow flowering in the future, good would come about because of what he had said to Anne. In the meantime he would pray more devoutly, strive to seek out the imperfection that had made him a poor instrument.

Holding his rosary under his cloak, Vincent began the Apostles' Creed. The cold rain ran down his neck.

II

THE BLOWS OF THE HAMMER

THE NEXT WEEKS would be the saddest of Vincent's life, not because of his physical suffering, although that was great, but because in his exile from Paris he would see the ghastly desolation of his country. The war had ceased to have any issues of right or wrong. Anne's stubborn indifference, Mazarin's clever manipulation of power, and the fickleness of Condé meant nothing in the provinces. All that the peasants knew was misery. Vincent, riding along the road to Villepreux, saw huts standing empty, with doors banging in the wind. Several times he came upon bodies lying where they had been pushed aside into the ditches, and he dismounted to say a prayer over them. There was nothing more he could do, for he had no spade for digging graves. Reaching the village, he sent a messenger back to Paris. All through the war he had kept his missionaries in the places where there was the greatest need for their spiritual attention. Now they must follow him to perform a corporal work of mercy, to bury the dead.

Vincent carried his sorrow inwardly in that late winter and spring of 1649. He was sixty-eight years old, a little, bent old man with a short white beard and a fringe of white hair edging down under his black skull cap. His teeth were all gone and his cheeks sunken, and his nose appeared larger than ever. The old wounds from his slave days were more troublesome in the cold weather, sometimes making him limp so badly that he had to be lifted on and off his horse. But his smile never wavered, and the light of love and kindliness never dimmed in his brown eyes. He had failed in his mission to the queen because of his own unworthiness, of that he was convinced, and God was now hewing away the imperfections.

"We are each a block of stone that God is going to form into a statue of his own design", Vincent told his Daughters at Villepreux. "First he takes the hammer and chips off the large chunks, sometimes striking so violently you'd think the whole block would fall apart.

Then he takes a smaller hammer, then a chisel, for the work becomes finer as it comes nearer to perfection. And that is how God forms us into what he wants. Look at us all! When God drew us to him, we were as rough and shapeless as the block of stone! So let us not complain about the blows of the hammer, my daughters. God permits us to suffer in order to bring us to perfection."

Until the missionaries arrived, Vincent remained in the village. Then, leaving them to hire gravediggers, if they could find them, he moved on toward Le Mans. The farther he traveled, the worse the suffering became. The peasants had long ago eaten every animal, even their horses, and now they were stripping bark from the trees, tearing grass out of the snow, and even eating straw mixed with clay into a sort of bread. Soldiers turned brigand were entering convents and abbeys, robbing and murdering, desecrating the Blessed Sacrament by trampling it underfoot. Some of the peasants, to save their lives, had banded together under a leader and then become outlaws themselves. Even Vincent was not safe from them. A gang of rowdies overtook him and surrounded him, shouting.

"Give us your horse, friend of the queen! You can get another from her!"

When the messenger from Saint-Lazare caught up with him, Vincent was plodding along on foot, with a heavy stick for a crutch. The messenger was Anthony Portail.

"Our farm at Orsigny is about to be pillaged, sir! Father Lambert is at his wits' end. If he goes to try to save the farm, the soldiers will surely move into Saint-Lazare! But Orsigny is important, too, for it furnishes us with our meat and grain. Father doesn't know what to do, Monsieur!"

Vincent listened attentively. Father Lambert, who was acting superior, was indeed between two fires.

"If the people of Paris are incensed against me, then it would only put Saint-Lazare in greater danger for me to return", he said. "Go back and tell Father Lambert to remain where he is, Anthony. Then ride to Orsigny yourself and see what you can do. It will be little, but try."

"Let me take you into Le Mans first, Father."

Vincent looked at the drooping horse. When people starved, the animals had even less.

"I'll not go into Le Mans, Anthony. We have another farm, you remember. Freneville. It may be in the same danger as Orsigny. I'll go there now. God be with you, my son!"

Vincent turned to trudge along the bleak road. Luckily Anthony had not remembered that Freneville was as far away as Le Mans. The pounding of the horse's hoofs on the frozen ground was like a drumbeat receding in the distance.

The farm at Freneville was deserted. Already the stables were empty, the grain bins despoiled of the wheat and corn that should be the seed for the new crop. The woodpile was gone. Out of the bleak gray sky snow was beginning to fall, skidding along ahead of a bitter wind. Vincent went into the hut where the caretaker's family had lived and propped the door shut with a stick. He had no food and nothing to burn in the fireplace. The wind, puffing down the chimney, sent the ashes of old fires out across the dirt floor. Kicked half under what remained of a bed was a cornhusk doll with charcoal eyes and a bit of soiled lace for a shawl.

Vincent picked up the pathetic toy. His little sister Mary used to play with dolls like that. His family had appealed to him for help, because even the Landes area had not escaped the desolation. He had hesitated to send them charity out of the confraternity funds. Then, luckily, he remembered a sum of a thousand sous that someone had given him long ago and that he had put away for some future purpose. He had not heard from John since sending the money. Perhaps the old home was as forlorn as this one.

Propping the doll carefully against the head of the bed, Vincent sat down, took out his breviary, and began to read.

By morning, as such news travels, the Daughters in the village heard that Monsieur Vincent had come to the farm, and two of them arrived with a little moldy bread and two withered apples.

"We have nothing better, Father", Francine apologized.

"It's far more than I need", Vincent smiled, and without another word about his own plight he began to ask about their work. It was the same story that might be repeated in every village of France—starving people and almost nothing to feed them.

"How God has blessed us!" Vincent exclaimed. "Where would these poor souls be without you?"

The snow was falling heavily when the girls left. They had begged Vincent to go back with them, but his legs were too painful for the long walk. Having gathered a little green wood, which was all they could find, and assuring him that they would be back soon, they were forced to leave him behind.

For over a month, cold and hungry, suffering too much to walk through the deep snow, Vincent remained at the farm. No one came near him but the Daughters, with their small supplies of food. When at last he was able to hobble into the village, he was so thin that the skin seemed to be stretched tight over his large skull. But his smile was bright until once again Anthony Portail arrived with news from Saint-Lazare.

The soldiers of Condé had finally entered Paris, and Saint-Lazare had been their first objective. A councillor who said he was acting with the approval of Parlement presented an order to search the premises. The remaining supplies of corn and flour were hauled away, and six hundred soldiers moved into the enclosure. Now, where prayers and psalms had been chanted, the rough talk of the soldiers echoed, and their coarse laughter took the place of the Company's silence. The few missionaries who had been at home were now prisoners in their cells, hungry, cold because the great pile of wood intended for the winter had been set afire by the soldiers in a night of triumphant revelry. Father Lambert begged that Vincent return to Paris.

Vincent shook his head sorrowfully. "I cannot do this, Anthony. My presence would only incite further violence, for the people have been led to believe that I am somehow to blame for their suffering."

"I'd like to run through the streets crying out what you have done for them!" Anthony blurted with usual fervor. "Without you, thousands would be dead! Don't they *know* that?"

"They only know what they have been told, my son. Don't blame them. Paris is better off without me now. Tell Father Lambert to go before Parlement and demand that the soldiers leave Saint-Lazare. And he must ask for a guard so they will not come back." Vincent paused, frowning. "I know we are locking the door after the stable is empty, but we can at least have the buildings left to us."

"But what of the hungry people who come to be fed, Monsieur?"

"Are there just as many as ever?"

"More! Two or three thousand a day."

"And there is no money, of course?"

"There is never any money, Monsieur", Anthony said with comic resignation.

"Then Father must ask the Ladies of Charity to aid him."

"They have already sold their jewels, Father!"

"They will sell more. God is blessing them in giving them such an opportunity for charity. They should thank him."

Anthony looked as if he doubted whether the Ladies might share this viewpoint. But Vincent was serenely confident.

"The funds will go further if Father Lambert sends the students to the country", he continued. "Divide them up among the confraternities where their help is needed the most. Keep only enough brothers at Saint-Lazare to staff the kitchen. Every mouthful of food must be given to the people. Now go, Anthony, and God be with you!"

Once again the hoofbeats of Anthony's horse died away like drums sounding a knell.

Vincent sat down in the middle of the cluttered soup kitchen to write two letters, one to the Pope, in which he recounted the terrible state of affairs in France and asked his intervention to end the war, the other to Anne of Austria. Great alms must come from somewhere, he told the queen. These were her people. She could save them from starvation.

The Holy Father did not reply. The queen gave an indolent order for money to be sent to Saint-Lazare, but she did not see that it was carried out. Not yet discouraged, Vincent went about the practical course of salvaging what was left at Orsigny. He had intended to stay at the farm, but a band of soldiers plundered the next farm, killing the cattle and murdering the peasants. Vincent gave no thought to his own safety. He did not, however, wish to lose the two hundred sheep and two horses that the raiders had overlooked at Orsigny. Alone, riding one of the horses, he set out for Richelieu, herding the sheep before him. His only real regret was that he had no dog to run nipping after the sheep that strayed. Since he must turn aside for each straggler, his progress was slow. The snow was too deep for the short legs of the sheep, and the animals were nearly exhausted when Vincent met the only traveler of the day, a woman who greeted him warmly.

"Monsieur Vincent, my friend! Don't you remember me, Marie of Saint-Denis? You preached a mission here for us!"

"Of course, of course", Vincent said, his eyes twinkling in spite of his fatigue. If he did not remember Marie, at least he remembered hundreds like her.

"Where are you going with the sheep, Monsieur? To Richelieu? You'll never get there with them! The road is full of soldiers. And the poor things, look at them lying in the snow. No, Monsieur, let me take care of them for you. We have a stout wall around our village and guards posted day and night. The soldiers leave us alone, I can tell you!"

Vincent could not refuse so generous an offer. In Marie's house, shared by her husband and seven children, he stayed for the night. There was a little food, and the fire leaped on the hearth.

"Stay with us until you are rested, Monsieur!" the woman begged. But Vincent climbed on his horse and rode away in the morning.

On the second of March he reached Le Mans, where there was famine as well as the plague. For two weeks he worked at the confraternity, helping to organize the distribution of food, cheering the Daughters and their priest-advisers, many of whom were already heroes, rejoicing over their unselfish service and humility. When he left Le Mans in the middle of March, the heavy snows had melted, and the Loire River was at flood stage. His horse stumbled, crossing at the ford, and Vincent was thrown into the water. He was saved from drowning only by being dashed against a large stump, to which he clung until he was rescued by a peasant. The horse was swept away by the flood.

Dripping though he was, Vincent would not halt his journey, so he thanked the peasant and tramped on his way. The sun was warm for March, and the wind whipped the water out of his cassock, but by night he was so exhausted and cold that, instead of sleeping as he had intended, in the open, he stopped at an inn. He was most reluctant to spend money on himself, but he had not eaten since leaving Marie's the night before.

The innkeeper received him gladly. He too had attended a mission preached by Monsieur Vincent. After supper the children gathered around, and Vincent instructed them while the parents and other guests listened. The little ones were so delightful that he felt rejuvenated, and he forgot his aching legs.

"The best room in the inn for you, Monsieur!" the keeper told him when the children had been carried off to bed.

The room was dirty and cold. Vincent, murmuring that it was much better than he needed, sat down to read his breviary by the light of the inadequate candle. Having finished, he had no more than lain down when a knock came at the door. Other guests had arrived, the innkeeper said, and he had no place to put them. Would Monsieur Vincent mind giving up his room?

"Not in the least, sir", said Vincent, and he picked up his ragged cloak and returned to the fireside. For the remainder of the night he sat reading his breviary and saying his prayers, while the innkeeper snored in the curtained bed in the corner.

At dawn, without breakfast, Vincent left the inn. The wind was cold again, spattering rain, and he trudged along so slowly that by noon he had barely reached Richelieu. His head was throbbing, and his eyes felt as if they were swollen in their sockets. He knew he was very ill. There was a confraternity in Richelieu, but no convent. The Daughters lived wherever they could in the poor homes. Vincent would not trouble them. Coming to a deserted house, he went inside and crawled into the rickety bed. The Daughters found him there in the morning.

Immediately a messenger was dispatched to Father Lambert at Saint-Lazare, for Monsieur Vincent was so ill that he knew no one, and it was feared he might be dying. Father Lambert sent a brother to care for the beloved superior, and he would come himself, he said, if Monsieur grew worse.

But as the days dragged by, the illness spent itself. Vincent's well-being was the affectionate concern of the entire town. Little bits of food were brought to tempt his appetite; the children picked the early flowers that bloomed on the grassy hillsides and set them shyly in cracked cups beside his bed. The women brought their needles and mended his ragged clothes, and the men stopped in the lengthening evenings to tell him the news they had heard during the day. Although the love and attention of the villagers was heartening, Vincent's improvement came only so far. His old wounds, festered again, would not heal.

Vincent was sitting in the sunshine of his doorway one day when a fine carriage drew up before him with a flourish, and one of the coachmen leaped down and presented him with a letter. It was from the queen. She had ordered him back to Paris.

He could not help the tears that fell on the worn old front of his cassock. His exile was over; he could return to his beloved Saint-Lazare. "I don't need a carriage", he told the coachman. "A horse, perhaps, because walking is impossible for me. But not a carriage."

The coachman in his lace and velvet was like a fine piece of china out of place in the muddy dooryard, but he spoke without a trace of condescension.

"The carriage is from the Duchess d'Aiguillon, Monsieur. A gift to you. Madame begs that you accept it."

Vincent, smiling, shook his white head. The duchess was a niece of the dead Richelieu, a charming and wealthy Lady of Charity, quite domineering in her own pretty way.

"I'll ride back to Paris in the carriage", he agreed. "After that, we shall see."

With the brother who was his nurse, Vincent climbed into the comfortable vehicle and urged the coachman to drive with all possible haste to Saint-Lazare.

The soldiers had gone and the students not yet returned, so the buildings were nearly empty on the warm afternoon when Vincent hobbled again across the courtyard of Saint-Lazare. Pigeons cooed in the lofts, and from the kitchens came the sound of a pot being scraped. It seemed impossible that this peaceful place could ever have known the violence of looting and burning. The clock in the chapel tower struck the hour. Humbly Vincent bowed his head. Always, no matter where he might be or in what conversation he might be involved, when he heard a clock strike he paused a moment for prayer. Tears ran down his cheeks now as he prayed in the quiet of Saint-Lazare. He was home again. And there was work to be done.

Paris, sick of evil, forgot the malicious gossip that had made a traitor of this most faithful of men, and once again Vincent was given his rightful place. His charity had kept thousands of people alive, the tongues now chattered. The devotion of his priests and Daughters to the poor could not have been inspired by any but a good man. They must have been mistaken about his desertion to the queen.

Furthermore, they still had need of his aid. Once more the soup line lengthened at the kitchen gate, and Monsieur Vincent became the strong pillar upon whom everyone leaned.

12

THE OPENING DOOR

VINCENT NEVER RETURNED TO HEALTH after his illness in the country, but he refused to let his physical infirmity interfere with his activities. He had seen at first hand the misery of the country people, and he knew now better than ever what must be done. The soup kitchens remained open, for the immediate need was to keep famine from sweeping the provinces, and there was still money to be begged from those whose fortunes remained. But a number of the wealthy who had contributed before were now destitute themselves. Their lands had been despoiled. The peasants who had supported the nobility with their taxes not only had no money but no grain for seed and no implements to work the soil. To start the industry that would eventually return France to normal living, it was necessary to get the farms back into production.

So Vincent set about the enormous task of obtaining and distributing the supplies needed by the peasants to plant another crop, an almost hopeless task, since there was so little to give them, and that little would be stolen by the first band of marauders who happened to come by. The war was not yet over. But Vincent persevered. The daughters of peasant families were gathered together for training as domestic servants, the boys apprenticed to tradesmen. For women who had been left alone he furnished flax and spinning wheels. He gave small salaries to priests who would otherwise have had to leave their parishes. Saint-Lazare itself became a refuge for priests, many of whom were the lazy and indifferent ones who had paid no heed to Vincent's urging that they perform their duties properly. Some of these would reform in the spiritual atmosphere of Saint-Lazare, others would not; but all were welcome and were treated alike. There was the work of maintenance for the convents and abbeys, another hopeless task because of the great number that had been plundered and the certainty that the same fate would befall them again and again until the war ended.

The future seemed to hold no promise that the war would ever end. The queen regent, the young king, and Mazarin were safely out of Paris and capable of remaining away indefinitely. Mazarin was enjoying the political juggling, which he was confident would result in victory for him. The queen, so long as she was entertained by her court, cared nothing about what might happen to her people.

Because the administration of all his great enterprises could be best accomplished from a central point, Vincent remained for the most part at Saint-Lazare, and the troubled and the suffering of the kingdom came to him. Upon his return from the country, the enormous old place had been almost deserted. Within a few weeks it was a teeming hive of activity. In the halls would be seen tradesmen and nobles, clergy and laity, nuns in patched habits and ladies in rather worn finery, all waiting for a word with Monsieur Vincent.

Brother Ducourneau respectfully scolded his superior at times for undertaking to solve all the problems of the world.

"Brother, Brother," Vincent would reply gently, "God in his goodness has given us a marvelous opportunity to serve these poor afflicted people. Come, who is next to see me?"

Often the next visitor would be a priest returned from one of the foreign missions, for the field had been widening ever since 1631, when Father du Coudray had gone to Rome to seek the approval of the Holy Father for the Congregation. The approval had not come through, but the priest had remained in Rome as a missionary. Soon requests came from Genoa and Turin for missionaries, and another from Corsica, where the priests were in the habit of saying Mass with a pistol hidden under the vestments, for in the heat of the vendettas the first victim would be the priest before the Blessed Sacrament. The crown of martyrdom was given to a lay brother in Ireland by Cromwell's spies. In Poland and Scotland there were Congregations of the Mission, and plans were being made to establish others in Tunis to aid the Christian slaves and in Madagascar among the people there.

From all of these places the priests or their messengers came to Saint-Lazare for reports and further instructions. The confraternities and mission parishes within the borders of France sent couriers with their requests and problems. Letters came daily from humble people. When a tailor who had once worked at Saint-Lazare wrote to ask for some needles that could be found only in Paris, Vincent gave the matter his personal attention. Every query received some sort of reply.

Underlying these concerns was the great anxiety Vincent felt for his country. By 1652 the war appeared to have reached a deadlock. The queen and Mazarin could hold out longer than the people, but hatred of the prime minister had become such a national issue that the whole country would die rather than submit. Vincent prayed long and fervently before taking the step which he saw as the only means of ending the strife. He had not been successful before in his mission to the queen, but he was convinced that it was because of his own unworthiness. In the months since then, he had suffered much and recognized his suffering as a purification. He could not rest unless he were to try again.

It was September when Vincent wrote his letter to Mazarin. He was careful not to offend, but he used the strongest terms possible. Paris was dying. Unless the illness could be healed soon, there would be nothing left to heal. The queen and the young king must return to the Palace of the City. But not Mazarin himself. Remain at a distance where he could be recalled by the king if need be—this was purely a sop to the cardinal's pride—but see that the queen regent and young Louis XIV come back with all speed.

Mazarin must have been furious, but he must also have seen the wisdom of Vincent's advice. He made no reply. In a few days, however, Anne and her son reentered Paris, to the cheering of the people, and the war was finally ended. The victory, in the long run, belonged to Mazarin. In the following February he once again took up his residence in the Royal Palace. Among his first acts was the dismissal of Vincent from the Council of Conscience.

Mazarin's revenge was not a bitter pill for Vincent. He never had wanted to sit on the Council. What did distress him was the chorus of praise for him rising all over Paris. Their beloved Monsieur Vincent, the people cried, had not only fed them through the terrible years of the Fronde but now he had brought about the end of the war. It did no good for him to insist that he had been merely the instrument of Providence. The chorus grew in volume, and Vincent's only escape was to remain as closely as he could within the confines of Saint-Lazare.

His physical condition was becoming more of a handicap day by day for the gentle old man. A long discussion back and forth with the Duchess d'Aiguillon about the gift of the carriage and horses had finally been ended by the archbishop of Paris, who put Vincent under obedience to use the conveyance. The horses, however, were used more for work about the grounds of Saint-Lazare than for drawing the carriage, and Vincent continued to hobble about the streets. He was smaller than ever now, his eyes twinkling brightly, his young spirit held in check only by the swollen legs that were his burden. The crown was not too far off in the future for Vincent de Paul.

The crowning of his work was to come in his lifetime. The approval of the Congregation of the Mission by the Holy Father, although several times within sight, had never come about. The Congregation was not a religious order, Vincent insisted. The priests were simply brought together to do a specific task, that of preaching missions. Rules were needed to bind them together. And rules, to Rome, meant a religious body. Vincent insisted that his priests were seculars. And so the long argument was spun out.

In 1651 it seemed to Vincent that a solution was at last in sight. The son of his old friend, de Gondi, had become archbishop of Paris. John Paul Francis de Gondi was the baby born during Vincent's early years as tutor to Madame's older sons. In his youth he had staged all sorts of rakish pranks to make his father see how unfitted he was for the priesthood. But the office of archbishop had belonged to the family since 1570, and there was no son but John to inherit it. So, with his tongue in his cheek, he had studied with flashes of brilliance for the priesthood. No sooner was he consecrated archbishop than he was arrested by Mazarin, who had no taste for so popular a man in power. Making a dramatic escape from prison and turning up finally in Rome, he was created Cardinal de Retz by the Holy Father and reinstated as archbishop. Vincent had immediate recourse to his sympathetic ear, but even with de Retz as spokesman the matter took time. Finally, through the archbishop's influence, Pope Alexander VII signed the papers that sanctioned the new Congregation, and on September 22, 1655, Vincent could announce to his priests assembled for retreat that they were now an official body of the Church.

"How God has blessed us!" he said to them. "He brought about the foundation of our little Company almost without our knowing it, and now he has made certain that it will continue in existence after we are gone." And tears of happiness ran down the old man's face.

It was not until the spring of 1658 that printed copies of the rules were ready to distribute to the Congregation. All of the priests and brothers returned to Saint-Lazare for the great event. Vincent was almost an invalid now. In addition to the ailments resulting from the wounds of his slave days, he had the fever that had come on after a runaway, when he had been thrown from his carriage. The Company, filing quietly into the big Common Room on that morning of May 17, knew that this might be the last assembly they ever would have with their beloved founder, whom they knew to be a saint. It was a scene none would ever forget. Sunshine streaming through a large window fell directly upon the chair where Vincent sat, a bent little man with white hair fringing his skull cap, his cassock the same old rusty black he had worn on the missions. His face was emaciated by illness, but when he spoke his voice was still strong and his subject matter as carefully put together as in the old days. His theme was the one they had heard a hundred times, "Only in having no will of our own can we follow God's will", but now it was the farewell message of a father to his sons. When he had finished, each priest and brother came forward to receive the little book of rules and Vincent's loving benediction, "May God bless you!"

In the same year, 1655, that saw the approval of Vincent's Congregation, Louise finally obtained sanction for her order. Since 1642, when Louise and two of her girls had been permitted to take perpetual vows, although only privately, the papal approval for the Daughters of Charity had been sought. As in the case of the Fathers, the organization was clearer to Vincent than to anyone else. He did not want his Little Sisters to be nuns, because nuns took vows that shut them into cloisters. Louise's girls must remain free to work among the poor. There was the question also of who should succeed, as someone inevitably must, as Sister Servant. Louise herself was a Lady of Charity, but she did not desire that the office of superior should be held in the future by a Lady of Charity. She was determined that it should not pass outside of her little group of Sisters. This was solved by giving the directorship to the General of the Congregation of the Mission and his successors, with the Sister Servant to be appointed by him from among the Sisters. The question of vows was resolved by having the members take them only for a year at a time. Louise was delighted, for the long delay had been exasperating to her. As the priests had done, all her Daughters assembled for the signing of their Deed of Foundation. Judging by the work they had accomplished in their years of existence, their number might be expected to be well up in the hundreds. Actually, thirty signed, nine making only an X because they could not write.

Through the next two years, from 1658 to 1660, Vincent's hand was still firmly upon all his great undertakings. But now the momentum had been gained that would carry them along without him. Like a hoop being guided by a runner, the hoop would continue smoothly on when another hand took over. This was what Vincent desired above all things. His work must not falter simply because he would be gone. In the time remaining to him he did his best to provide directions for the future of the vast network of undertakings that God had wrought through him. There were the confraternities, which still were of vital service, for France would always have its poor. The missions must be preached and good priests sent into parishes where there were none to carry on the revival started by the missionaries. The Tuesday Conferences were rejuvenating the priesthood. There were the Visitation Nuns, who must still be directed by the superior of the Congregation. Retreats for laymen had been started at Saint-Lazare, with several hundred men coming at a time to be housed and fed for a week. Since no charge ever was made, some came who had no other interest than the good food.

"What does it matter?" Vincent answered the complaint of the brother in charge of supplies. "Perhaps a few will take the sermons to heart. As for those who do not, at least they have given us the opportunity for charity."

For those who could not help themselves, Vincent had founded the shelters suited to their needs: orphanages, the Little Houses where for the first time the insane were humanely treated, the Hospice of the Holy Name of Jesus for respectable old people, houses for beggars, and hospitals for the galley slaves. As royal almoner, Vincent had brought about lasting reform in the prisons.

In addition to these concerns he was occupied with his Congregations in foreign countries and with the Ladies of Charity, who were still active and demanding his attention. Reports from all of these widely scattered enterprises poured in to Saint-Lazare, and Vincent treated each as if it alone were the important thing.

"The good which God wishes to be done is done without our thinking about it", he wrote in a letter. "If he made use of us in bringing into existence some of the things he wanted done, he sometimes did it without our even knowing that a beginning was being made, and it was unnecessary for us to concern ourselves as to where the work was going to lead."

Now it seemed that not only were there no more beginnings to be made, but the final curtain was about to fall on all the opening scenes. In the spring of 1660, Vincent's two best-loved friends, Louise le Gras and Anthony Portail, died within a few weeks of one another.

"Perhaps they will open the door for me", Vincent said to the brother who nursed him.

He had not wanted to be moved out of the bare little cell that was his only home. But there was no way to heat it, and the doctor finally grew insistent that Vincent have a few of the comforts permitted to all the sick. Over his protests the brothers moved him to a room with a fireplace, and adjoining it they fitted up a chapel where he could hear the Mass he was no longer able to say. Patiently he endured their care.

"My sufferings are nothing compared to our Lord's", he would say. "I deserve none of the kindness that was denied him."

Vincent never had allowed women to come into his cell. Even when he received one of the Ladies of Charity in a reception room, a brother had always to remain outside of the open door. But now the Daughters, grieving for Louise, begged Vincent to see them. He could not refuse. Twice in July, and for the last time on the twenty-fourth of August, they crowded into his little room. There was no tinge of farewell in his last words to them. He blessed each and spoke as a loving father, and they filed quietly out.

When the Ladies of Charity heard that the Daughters had been to see Vincent, they asked for an audience also. They had been the backbone of his charities, and again he could not refuse. Some of them wept as they left; but their most vivid memory would be of a smiling, tired, but content old man who had prayed and labored his way to sainthood.

On September 27, 1660, at four o'clock, which was his hour for rising, the shepherd boy who had grown up to feed the flocks of France died in his sleep, his passing as humble as his life had been. Seated in his chair, wearing the old cassock and skull cap, with the name of Jesus on his lips, Vincent de Paul passed through the opened door.

The fathers and brothers knew he was a saint. None had seen very far into the inner existence of this man who had lived so close to God, for it had been his humble way to hide every grace and virtue. For himself he wanted nothing. For God, everything. That was the mark of his saintliness.

Rich and poor crowded into the church of Saint-Lazare and filed past the bier in such numbers that the brothers who were the guard of honor were sometimes hard put to maintain decent order. But no one was turned away. Monsieur Vincent would not have wanted it. His life had been spent in the service of God through the poor. To the outpourings of love and praise, to the grandiose dignity of his funeral, which was attended by royalty, he would only have said humbly, "Lord, I am not worthy."

In 1737, the seal of canonization was set before the name of Vincent de Paul, saint of charity. The man who on earth had counted himself among the last had come into his rightful place among the first in heaven.

Author's Note

Out of the confusion of civil war, poverty, and religious double-talk that pervaded France in the 1600s, Vincent de Paul rises as the great man of the century. The son of a peasant, never forgetful of his humble birth, he pursued a straight way of simplicity that made him the friend of beggars and the adviser of royalty. To study the life of Vincent is to understand better the neglected virtue of patience. "In God's good time" was the watchword of his work; but once convinced that the time had come, nothing could deter him. His point of view was often far ahead of his day: the beggars of Paris should work for their keep; the old and infirm should be housed and cared for decently, orphans rescued and taught, poverty met with charity organized to give enough and yet conserve for harder times. "The poor are our masters", he told his Little Sisters, and under the guidance of Louise de Marillac he sent them out, with the streets for their cloister walk and their own virtue as their only barricade against temptation. Slow to take form, magnificent in the clearness of its purpose, the Congregation of the Sisters of Charity is one of the many gifts of Vincent to our modern world.

In the limited space of this book, only the barest

outline of so full a life can be given. Saint Francis de Sales and the Sisters of the Visitation, the foreign missions and the Council of Conscience, the wide fields covered by the Ladies of Charity and the mission priests—all these would make another book. This little volume is therefore only a bow to the great and humble man.

For my information on Vincent de Paul, the following books have been my main sources:

The Life and Works of Saint Vincent de Paul, by Pierre Coste, C.M. (translated by Joseph Leonard, C.M.). Westminster, Maryland: Newman Press, 1952.

The Heroic Life of Saint Vincent de Paul: A Biography, by Henri Lavedan (translated by Helen Younger Chase). London: Longmans Green, 1929.

Apostle of Charity, the Life of St. Vincent de Paul, by Theodore Maynard. New York: Dial Press, 1939.

Vincent de Paul, Priest and Philanthropist, 1576–1660, by Emma Katharine Sanders. London: Heath Cranton Ouseley, 1913.